Also by Aruda Hanna Wilson

Sea Dreams

The Weeping Crystal

Other Books from Deer Hawk Enterprises:

Heart of Dixie by Ronald Polizzi

The Deception by Aurelia Sands

Flights of Phantasy

Aruda Hanna Wilson

Aruda Hanna Wilson

Deer Hawk Enterprises
Florida

Flights of Phantasy
Copyright © 2009 by Aruda Hanna Wilson

All rights reserved. No part of this publication may be reproduced, stored in a retrieval system or transmitted in any form or by any means, electronic, mechanical, photocopying, recording or otherwise without prior written permission of the copyright owner except for excerpts quoted in the context of reviews.

This is a work of fiction. Names, characters, places and incidents portrayed in this book are either the product of the author's imagination or are used fictitiously. Any resemblance to actual persons, living or dead, events or locales is entirely coincidental.

Cover design and illustrations by:
Bernadette "Teri" Norman

Layout by:
Aurelia Sands

Published by:
Deer Hawk Enterprises
www.deerhawkpublications.com
Library of Congress Control Number:
2009926420

These stories are dedicated to my family. To my husband, Dennis, who is probably due for sainthood by now, thank you for putting up with me. To my three lovely children: Theresa, Glenn, and Brian, thanks for the insanity that made writing possible, and finally, thank you to Storm, my cat, for all the ideas she gave me, and Bat, the dog, for reminding me it's dinner time.

Some of these stories were written a long time ago: *The Game* was written in the heyday of the Nintendo game system (the first one), with the tiny pixilated characters.

Most Famous was based on my grandfather, and last time I was home, Woods Rodgers Drive was still as narrow and crowded with vendors hawking their wares as ever. The bar in the story, *The Little Brown Jug,* was also still standing.

The Girl Who Could Fly came into being when I realized how many women truly believed that they could fly when they were children.

Mama's Stories is a group of short stories based on the tradition of storytelling. Before television, every culture had its storyteller: A person who entertained and educated the next generation. Mama Sistella is the storyteller of her town.

The Border is a social commentary on modern society, where the past is being lost to the future for present gain.

The other stories were written more recently and with no ulterior motives that I am aware of. The newest two are *The Truth*

Behind the Madness; and *The Madness Begins*. After *Sea Dreams* was published, I received numerous requests for more information about the Lantian people. Those two represent another part of that story.

Welcome to my phantasies, I hope you enjoy the tour.

Aruda

The Border

Judith stared at her father in shock. He wasn't lying, but the way he was telling the truth made it all sound so crazy. She knew she had to do something.

Grandmother just sat in her chair and listened while her only child told a judge that she was crazy. Judith knew why her father was doing it: He wanted The Border. He would take the land, subdivide it, build little square houses, and destroy the trees out back of the house.

Judith wanted to jump up and scream, but if she did, the judge would ignore her. He would think she was just a child and not pay any attention to what she had to say.

Judith glanced at her grandmother, and saw that the older woman was watching her with a slight smile. Judith nodded. She knew what she had to do.

"Your Honor," Judith stood up, ignoring her mother's tugging at her shirt. Her father turned and glared at her.

The judge peered at her over the top of his glasses. "Young Lady, unless you have something to say that is pertinent to this trial, I suggest you sit down."

"I do have pertinent information, Your Honor."

Her father's lawyer jumped up, "Your Honor, I object. This child does not understand what is going on. She loves her grandmother and therefore accepts as normal, behavior that adults know can be dangerous."

The judge glanced at Judith, then sighed, "Is what you have to say important?"

Judith looked him in the eye. "Your Honor, I'm young; but I'm not a child. I'm sixteen-and-a-half, I have passed two years of college, and all my instructors think I am quite mature for my age. My father's lawyer is correct, I do love my grandmother; and I don't see anything dangerous in her behavior. That's for you to decide. There is certain information, however, that I think you should see before you make this decision."

Judith drew a deep breath, hoping she sounded intelligent and mature. She also hoped the judge decided quickly, her legs were trembling so much she was afraid she would fall.

The judge nodded, "This is irregular, but I think I want to hear what the young lady has to say. I am going to call a fifteen minute recess while I speak to her in my chambers." The judge smiled and left the courtroom.

*****

Judith sank gratefully into the large, leather chair facing the judge's desk. She frowned while she tried to figure out how to begin.

"Your Honor, my name is Judith Leiu Howard. I am named after my grandmother."

The judge nodded encouragingly and Judith took a deep breath.

"Your Honor, my father wants you to make him my grandmother's guardian. They say she is senile because she refuses to allow my father to sell her home."

"That's the property known as The Border, isn't it?" The judge asked. "Isn't it true that she refuses to sell the property because elves and fairies live in the woods out back of the house?"

Judith laughed. "Your Honor, the land has been in my family ever since we first came to this country. It has always belonged to the women. There is a special legal document that says so. They had to make a legal document, because, in the old days, women couldn't own property." Judith blushed, "But you know that, you're a judge."

The judge laughed, "Yes, Judith, I know that. What's your point?"

"The point, Your Honor, is that in eighteen months, ownership of that land comes to me, and I don't want my father to be trustee for the land. If you decide that Grandmother needs a guardian, fine; but The

Border and the trust fund to maintain it must not be placed in my father's hands."

"Because you want to protect the elves and fairies? Young Lady, don't you realize that such tales are not true? Your stand against your father is weakened by the reasons you have for protecting the land."

"Your Honor," Judith frowned and shook her head dismissively. "Do you think my grandmother and I are such fools? The Border is a wildlife sanctuary; it is protected under the Federal Wetland Act.

"Also, growing out in the back of the house is a stand of some of the oldest trees in the nation. I know, because verification came in the mail just today." Judith smiled triumphantly as she handed the judge the official Forestry Department envelope.

"Why doesn't your father know all this?" The judge asked, frowning.

"My father hasn't been to The Border in over twenty years. Whenever Grandmother comes to visit us, he always tries to convince her to sell. He never listens to anything Grandmother or I try to tell him.

The Border

"Grandmother got so frustrated with him one day that she asked him where all the fairies and elves would go if she cut down the woods out back, and sold the land."

Judith sighed, "My grandmother and I both love my father very much, but, Your Honor, sometimes he can be so dense."

The judge coughed suddenly and turned away. When he turned back to Judith, he was rubbing his chin. "Well, Young Judith Leiu Howard, I thank you for all the information you have given me. Now, why don't you go on back to the courtroom? I'll be there in a minute."

Judith sat next to her mother and waited for the judge to appear. She ignored her mother's frantic whispers and her father's scowl.

The judge stacked all his notes neatly in front of him, took a deep breath, and winked at Judith.

"Well, I have come to a decision." The judge paused, and Judith glanced at her grandmother, who was sitting very still. She wondered how her grandmother could act so calm under the circumstances.

"Judith Leiu Howard Senior does indeed need a guardian." The judge smiled grimly, "I do not think, however, that her son is the correct person for the job. So, until her granddaughter, Judith Leiu Howard Junior, is old enough to assume that position, I remand Judith Leiu Howard Senior to the custody of all the elves and fairies living at The Border. After everything the two Judiths have done to protect them, they can surely take care of one old woman for a few years.

"This case is dismissed." The judge stood and turned to Judith's father. "Next time you come before me for any reason, make sure you have ALL the facts in your case."

*****

Judith and her grandmother sat on the back porch of The Border, drinking lemonade and watching the sunset. It was the perfect way to end a long day.

Her father was furious.

The Border

When Judith announced that she was going to spend the rest of the summer with her grandmother, her father said, "Good riddance!" and slammed the door behind her.

Judith sighed, "Well, Grandmother, it worked. There is no way that Dad can sell The Border: Not now."

Her grandmother nodded, then pointed to the far corner of the trees. Judith turned to look and caught a fleeting glimpse of a white horse. One breath, and it was gone.

Judith blinked. "Grandmother, I didn't know you had horses."

Her grandmother smiled in contentment, "I don't."

"But I just saw, at least I think. . ." Judith paused in confusion.

"Hush, Granddaughter. You can see many wonderful things once you learn to watch in silence."

The young Judith sat, holding her cold glass in her hands as the sun slowly slid behind the horizon. She felt very proud of what she had done this past year. All her plans to protect The Border, with the help of the federal government, had worked. The woods were safe for as long as the government existed. After that, well, that would be a problem for another Judith, in another time.

The Border was more than just the name of her family's estate. It really was a border. Grandmother said that it was one of the last remaining places on the planet where the land of Dreams and the land of Men still met.

The Girl Who Could Fly

"Mose, would you believe that years ago I could fly?"

The tall, thin man lounging on her couch shook his head, "You still having that dream about flying when you were a kid?"

"Yeah. I woke up last night in a cold sweat. I wish I knew why that dream bothered me. I haven't had a good night's sleep since my vacation."

Mose stared intently at the hole in the toe of his size thirteen sneakers, "Take another one."

Jan, ran her fingers through her short, brown hair. "Why are you still wearing those old sneakers?"

Mose's gray eyes laughed at her, "Because they are comfortable. Stop trying to change the subject. Go visit your hometown; you haven't been back in ten years. I think that's what your dream is all about."

"I don't want to go back." Jan pouted, her brown eyes dark with remembered pain, "You don't know what it was like being different. My parents tried to keep me hidden so no one would know about me."

"Jan, they were doing their best to protect you."

"Yeah, you've told me that before. I still don't believe you. I never had a normal life until you rescued me from that place."

Mose sighed, "Jan, there is nothing normal about your life even now. You have money to spare, but you never go anywhere unless it's on psychic business. I handle all your money; I even do your grocery shopping for you. All you've done is exchange one set of jailers for another. That's not the reason I brought you to America."

"You brought me here because you could use my skills to make a fortune."

"Well, I shared it with you, didn't I?" Mose stretched, "I repeat. Take a real vacation."

"I just came back from a vacation."

"I wouldn't call going to a psychic convention in 'Frisco a vacation. You spent more time with the scientists who were testing you than you did resting."

"How do you know what I did, you didn't go with me. George wouldn't let you out of his sight that long."

"Not quite right. I couldn't leave George alone that long." A wicked grin creased Mose's long, thin face.

"Same thing," Jan snapped. She hated talking about George. Anyone who took Mose's attention from her was, in her mind, an enemy.

"Okay, so what did you do on your vacation?"

"I went to see a psychic. I wanted to find out why my powers were becoming so erratic."

"Oh, that's rich, Jan. I swear your thinking is warped. What did she say?"

"Madam Zelda told me to get in touch with my past so that I could resolve the problem of my future."

Mose covered his eyes and slid further down on the couch. "You went to see a psychic called 'Madam Zelda'? Gods, Jan, you're the best proven psychic in the nation. Law enforcement agencies all over the country come to you for help. You've made both of us rich on the stock market; and you go to see some broad with a phony name like 'Madam Zelda'? I don't believe it."

"Mose, for the last year, my psychic powers have been sporadic. I was worried about it."

"I keep telling you; you need a good vacation and a good man, not necessarily in that order."

"Moses Krew!"

"Yeah, all right, so you have been dreaming you could fly. Half the women I know believe they could fly when they were kids. Maybe it's some kind of female genetic memory."

"Do you really believe that?"

"No, I just said it to make you feel better."

"Gods, why do I put up with you?" Jan flopped down on the couch next to Mose.

"I'm your best friend." Mose smiled at the slender woman beside him.

"You're my only friend."

Mose reached over and gathered Jan in his arms, "That's the point I was trying to make earlier. You need a social life. Get out, meet people, and stop worrying. I'll still love you even if you lose your powers. We're both rich enough to retire in comfort."

Jan snuggled into his arms for a moment, then pushed him away. "What would George think if he saw us now?"

Mose gave her a strange look, "I don't believe George thinks."

"Mose, that's a terrible thing to say."

"Why are you so worried about George's feelings? You won't even come to my house to meet him. Look, why don't we saddle up those two monsters of yours and go for a ride? Take your mind off things for a while."

Jan smiled, "Adam and Eve are not monsters, they're Percherons."

"Yeah, that's what I said: Monsters." Mose mumbled as Jan went to dress for the ride.

*****

"Mose, can you come over?"

"Jan, it's two in the morning."

"I know, but I need to talk to you."

"Okay, give me fifteen minutes."

Half an hour later, Mose was sitting in his favorite position on her couch, a cup of coffee in his hand. "Okay, what was so important that you had to see me now?"

Jan frowned and leaned her head against the cool, dark pane of the large window in her living room. "I had a dream I was out riding and the day was real misty. I had just decided to turn back, when the mist parted and I saw a ring of strange trees. They glowed with a kind of bluish light. I'd never seen trees like them before. Beyond the trees was a dark, rocky beach; you know, dark sand, gray water, black rock. The whole scene should have been tranquil, even peaceful, but it wasn't. The air was heavy with menace, as if something evil and dangerous was waiting just outside the ring of trees.

"There was a man sitting under one of the trees. All the malice in the night seemed to focus on him. I sensed that he was injured and needed help, and that he couldn't face the danger in the condition he was in. The man wasn't human. There wasn't anything in his looks that said he wasn't, it was just a feeling that I had.

"I rode into the clearing, climbed off Adam's back and started a fire. Somehow, Adam's saddlebag was filled with food. I didn't think it odd: I just fixed some soup and gave it to the man. I pulled out a first-aid kit, cleaned his wounds, and bandaged them.

"Now, this was weird: I spent days there, taking care of him and not one word was spoken. Then, a group of soldiers in old-fashioned armor rowed up to the beach in a small boat. There was a tall woman with long, dark hair in the boat with them. When she stepped on the beach and lifted her arms in greeting, it felt as if all the evil that surrounded us drew back a bit. The soldiers hailed the man. He handed me a staff made from the wood of those strange trees before he ran down the beach to join the others."

Mose sighed and ran his fingers through his tousled black hair, "You got me out of my warm bed for a dream?"

"Mose, when I woke up, I was in the stable with Adam and Eve, my night dress was dirty and torn, and Adam was all lathered like he'd been ridden hard and fast for a long time, and I was holding this." Jan held up a smooth, three-foot-long piece of polished wood.

"Is this something I should call the cops and warn them about?"

"No." She answered absently. Jan opened the front door, walked onto the porch, and pushed the staff into the ground. She shivered and stepped back into the house.

Mose watched her, a worried look in his eyes. "Who was the man? Did you recognize him?"

"No. I told you, he wasn't even human. It's just that the dream was so real, I could smell the sea, taste the bite of the smoke from the fire. It's as if I was really there." She shivered and closed the door.

"Maybe you were. You've had this kind of dream before. It's what you do for a living. So, what's the real problem?"

"I don't know. The fact that I woke up in the stables and the condition Adam was in, has me worried."

"You sure that's all?"

"Uh huh."

"Did this dream scare you?"

"Not really. There was a job to be done; I did it; end of dream. What bothered me was waking up in the stable and being alone." She walked over to Mose, and took a sip of his coffee.

"Want me to stay with you for a while?"

"What about George?"

"It's close enough for me to check on George every day without problems."

"Then yes, please. I would like the company."

*****

On the fourth morning, Jan was not in her room when Mose went to wake her. A quick check of the stables showed that Eve was missing. As Mose made his way back to the house, he heard the thunder of hooves. He turned and watched as Jan rode her horse swiftly into the yard.

Mose caught Jan as she slid from Eve's back, "Are you all right?"

Jan stared at him blankly for a moment, "Yes."

"Where have you been?"

"Another dream, I think. It had to have been." She shook her head. "Let's go inside. After I clean up, I'll tell you about it."

Mose was waiting with coffee when Jan entered the room. She took her cup and sat down with a sigh.

"Rescued another warrior?"

She smiled, "No. This time it was a woman and child. I was on top of a hill. The trees and the beach from my other dream were behind me. In front of me stretched a low, rocky plain. There was a woman with a bundle on her back running toward me. Behind her were mounted men, armed with swords. The men were making a game of the chase. As the woman stumbled toward me, I knew I had to help her. It wasn't until she was up on Eve's back behind me that I realized the bundle she carried was a child.

"'Where do you want to go?' I asked.

"'The mountains. We'll be safe there,' she said.

"'Why are the soldiers chasing you?' I asked

"She said they wanted to kill her baby and when I asked her why, she looked at me very strangely and said 'She's a flier. All fliers must die. It's the law, you know that.'

"I started to explain that I didn't know anything about her world at all, but for an instant, I knew exactly what she was talking about."

"Then what happened?"

"Nothing. I put her and the baby down at the foot of the mountains, then I woke up in the yard with you helping me off Eve's back."

"You didn't get much of the atmosphere in this dream. The last one had more detail didn't it?"

"Yeah, well, I wasn't in this dream as long. There was a sense of urgency too, so I didn't have much time to absorb the surroundings. One thing though, the trees were the same, they were weird, and glowed with a sort of bluish light."

"Now what?"

"I don't know. There's still more to happen. I just wish I knew if it will be in 'real time' or 'dream time'."

*****

It was a week later that the police asked Jan to help them find a five-year-old girl who had been kidnapped.

Jan stopped suddenly when she and Mose entered the police station.

"What's the matter with you?" Mose whispered.

"That couple over there: I know them. Mose, they're the two people I helped in my dream."

"Jan, they're the child's parents. I thought you said the people in your dream weren't human. Those two sure look human to me."

"But they're not! Can't you see? Look closely."

Mose shook his head, but before he could answer, Jan shouted, "NO! Mose, take me home!" She ran out of the building, Mose close on her heels.

"Okay, Babe, you want to tell me what this is all about?"

"I know where the child is. I saw her just as plain as I do you. She was in that old, abandoned building not far from our place. Mose, she has escaped from the kidnappers."

"Great, I'll drive you there and we'll pick her up. The cops are right behind us, so there will be no problems."

"Mose, take me home. I'll ride Adam across the fields. Give me a few minutes' head start, then bring the police by road."

"Jan, what's going on?"

"Mose, that child escaped because she flew out of a third-story window. Right now, she's hiding in an old oak tree, but if I can't get her down before the cops arrive, there are going to be some very awkward questions asked."

Mose nodded and turned into her driveway, "Get out. I'll think of something to keep the police busy for a while. Be careful."

"Thanks." She frowned briefly at the vaguely familiar sapling by her door. *When did that get there?* she wondered as she ran toward the stable.

Jan didn't take the time to saddle Adam; she climbed on his back and rode swiftly away.

When she reached the place the girl was hidden, Jan jumped from Adam's back. "You can come down now. I've come to take you home."

There was a long moment of silence, then the child's voice floated down, "What took you so long?" The leaves rustled and the girl glided through the air and landed not far from where Jan was standing.

Something snapped in Jan's mind. Jan knelt beside the child and shook her gently, "Look at me; look-at-me."

When the child's eyes met hers, Jan hissed, "You cannot fly. Do you hear me? You-can-not-fly."

"But…"

"No!" Jan interrupted, tears running down her face, "Look at me. You cannot fly."

She remembered what happened after her flight to the porch. Her mother said and did the same thing to her. For her safety, for her life, she had to forget.

"I can't fly?" The child repeated softly, and Jan hugged her close.

"Thank you."

Jan glanced up to see the child's mother standing over them. The woman took her child, and her eyes, filled with pain and understanding, met Jan's.

*****

Mose found Jan hours later sitting in her dark house, "Hey, Babe, you all right?"

"I took something very precious from that child today. I took away a memory, a talent, a heritage, and I had no right: None at all."

"You saved her life."

"No, I took her dream away. She'll never fly again. She won't even remember; none of us ever does. She won't remember until her own daughter flies, then she'll obey some genetic compulsion and take that gift away from her child."

"Like I said, you saved her life. How long do you think she would last in our society if anyone ever found out she could fly? Maybe, sometime in the future, it will be safe, but for now, no way. You saved her life."

He watched her think over his words, then walked to her front door and opened it.

"Cheer up kid, I brought someone over to meet you."

"I'm not in the mood for company, Mose."

"Oh, but this is a very special someone. Since you wouldn't come over to meet George, I figured I'd bring him over to meet you."

Jan closed her eyes tightly, only to open them again as her face was washed by a large, rough tongue. She found herself staring into the soft, brown eyes of the largest Doberman she had ever seen.

"George?"

Mose laughed softly, "George."

"Hi George," Jan whispered, burying her face in the dog's neck. "Mose?"

"Yeah, Babe?"

"Did you know that when I was a child I could fly?" She smiled

"Yep."

"I've been silly, haven't I? When one door closes, another opens. When my mother took the gift of flight away, I received an extra sense in return. That child, well, she'll be all right. "

Jan sat back as George pushed his large head close to her. "I'm going home for a few days. I need to revisit the old neighborhood, and make my peace with the past." She nuzzled the dog's soft fur, "Come with me, you and George?"

"Just name the day."

Mose watched her for a while, "Jan?"

"Ummm?"

"What about your dreams? Are they over?"

Jan, who was busy scratching George's ears, gave Mose a puzzled look, "What dreams?"

Mose looked at her, frowned, then shrugged. He already forgot his question.

*****

Outside, the air shifted, and the small sapling in Jan's front yard briefly shimmered with a soft blue halo, then it too, forgot.

The Game

"Mr. And Mrs. Franklin," Doctor Gaud paused.

"Tommy's dying, isn't he?" The woman on the other side of his desk asked him.

"Yes," Dr. Gaud said softly.

"How long does he have?"

"A few days, two weeks at the most."

Mrs. Franklin took a deep breath and squeezed her husband's hand. "Will he be in pain?"

"No." Dr. Gaud said, relieved she was not being hysterical. He never knew how to deal with screaming parents.

"Does Tommy know?" Mrs. Franklin's soft voice interrupted his thoughts.

"I told him last night that he was going home." Dr. Gaud deliberately misinterpreted her question.

"Does Tommy know he's going to die?"

"We haven't told him. He knows he's getting weaker and has been here long enough to figure out what's going to happen. Mrs. Franklin, all we can do here at the institute is keep the children's morale up. We try not to discuss any subject that will depress them. If you feel it wise to tell Tommy he has only a few weeks left, that's your prerogative. We strongly advise against it."

Mrs. Franklin gave the doctor a look of disdain.

"Do you know what's wrong with him?" Mr. Franklin asked before his wife could say anything else.

"No. All our efforts for the last four years have not revealed the source of Tommy's illness." Dr. Gaud leaned back in his chair. "We don't know what caused healthy nine and ten-year-old children to suddenly become sick and die within a year.

We don't know why Tommy and a few others have survived almost four years. We also don't know why the disease is suddenly tapering off. So far this year, we have only had two new cases worldwide. We think whatever it was, has now mutated to a non-virulent strain."

Dr. Gaud ran his hands across his face. He was tired and depressed. As a scientist, he found his inability to isolate the cause of this worldwide illness depressing. Most of all, he hated having to admit his ignorance to his patients' parents.

*****

In a bare hospital room down the hall, three young people talked softly. They were discussing Dr. Gaud in a way he would have found most disconcerting.

"Either he's stupid or he thinks we are." Rudy said flatly.

Angela sniffed, "They don't think about us at all. We're just experiments to them, not real people. If any of the adults in this place ever thought about it, they would realize we figured out what was happening a long time ago."

"That's not fair, Angela, some of the nurses really care. They have no way of knowing that we overheard them talking almost two years ago." Tommy sat up carefully, wincing in pain, "I don't care what Doctor Gaud says. I may be going home because he and his staff can't do anything else for me, but I'm not going to die; not until I'm ready to."

Rudy and Angela stared at their roommate. Tommy was pale and thin. His hair hung limply across his skull and his brown eyes were hard with determination. If any of them could beat this disease, it would be Tommy.

"Are you going to get better?" Angela whispered.

"No." Tommy shook his head. "None of us are ever going to get better. Nobody knows what's wrong with us. No one knows what makes us so tired that at last we just go to sleep and never wake up. Until they find out what's wrong, they won't be able to cure it. The three of us, we have survived the longest and no one knows why.

I mean, we have been here for four years and are still alive."

Rudy stared at the white ceiling for a while, then he took a deep breath. "We play the game," he whispered.

The room was silent. Outside the door, the three children heard the soft sounds of the nurses' feet hurrying up and down the hall.

"Wizard," Angela breathed.

"Warrior," Tommy whispered.

"Thief," Rudy frowned. "We live in the game. The game keeps us alive."

"I believe we can live in the game." Tommy said softly, glancing at the door of their room.

"How?" Rudy demanded.

Tommy shrugged, then winced at the pain it caused. "I don't know how." He lay back down and gave a tired smile. "We will each have to discover that for ourselves."

*****

When Tommy's parents came to get him early the next morning, he was dressed and waiting in his small wheelchair. He smiled bravely and went along with the pretense that he was being sent home because he was getting better.

"Tommy, we have a surprise for you."

Tommy glanced at his mother. Whatever the surprise was, she was nervous about it. "What?" he asked.

"Well, we changed your room around a bit."

Tommy smiled. His mother remembered how stubborn he could be about changes. He never wanted her to redecorate his room, always insisting that he liked it just the way it was.

"I just knew you couldn't be trusted," he teased. "As soon as I turned my back, you had to change something. Whatever are we going to do with her, Dad?"

"Well, we could always trade her in for a newer model," Tommy's dad said with a straight face.

"Yeah," Tommy said thoughtfully, "But we've had her for so many years now, what sort of trade-in would we get?"

Tommy's dad grinned. "I guess we better keep her."

Tommy, a look of fake disgust on his face, nodded. His mother laughed.

Tommy smiled, "It's good to hear you laugh." He sighed in mock exasperation. "I suppose I'll just have to wait until we get home to see what you've done."

*****

Tommy's mother made him close his eyes before she opened his bedroom door and his father wheeled him into the room.

"Okay, Tommy, open your eyes now."

Tommy opened his eyes and gasped in delight. His mother had removed the outside wall of his room and replaced it with glass. Large, sliding glass doors led to a small, screened-in patio with a table and three chairs. Outside the patio, trees and flowers bloomed. A birdbath and feeder sat in the middle of the miniature garden. As Tommy watched, four birds flew down and began bathing.

"Do you like it?" his mother asked nervously.

The Game

"Oh! Mom, Dad, it's perfect! Thank you." Tommy laughed as he watched the birds.

He glanced around the room. Nothing else had changed except his old bed, which was replaced by a hospital bed. Tommy sighed, and his father, following his gaze, smiled.

"It's an electric bed, Son. If you want to play your video games, all you have to do is press the button and the bed moves up into a sitting position. When you get tired, press the button again and you will be lying down. It gives you some freedom until you can get around on your own."

"Mom, Dad, I know."

"Know what?" his father asked quietly.

"I know that Dr. Gaud sent me home to die."

"No!"

"Mom, don't. I promise you I'm not going to die as soon as the doctor thinks. I have something I want to do first." Tommy reached out and took his mother's hand. "I just wanted to let you know that I knew.

This way, we don't have to pretend with each other."

Tommy's mother squeezed his hand and his father took his other hand.

"No matter what happens, Tommy," his father said, "I want you to know that we are proud to have you as our son. We wouldn't trade you for anyone else."

Tommy blinked back tears and smiled. "Besides, Dad, in my shape, what sort of trade-in allowance would you get?"

The three of them laughed softly, then Tommy's parents helped him undress and put him to bed.

*****

The next morning, Tommy pulled out his favorite video games. He, Rudy and Angela played this game in their heads for three years, each of them taking a different character. When they first got sick, these games were the biggest role-playing games in the country.

Now, as he replayed them, he felt as if something was missing. Tommy frowned when he finished *Sky Dream* and started in on the second game of the series, *Land Dream*.

"Tommy?"

Tommy glanced up and saw his mother watching him from the door.

"Yeah, Mom?"

"Are you replaying those *Dream* games?"

"Yeah."

"Your father and I wrote the company and told them how you and your friends loved their games and how sick you were. We hoped that they would send one of their writers to the hospital to see you three. Instead, they sent you their new game. It's the last one of the series. We decided to wait until you got home to give it to you, so here it is."

Tommy took the small box from his mother and read the title of the new game. "*The Last Dream*. Thanks, Mom." He said absently. Excitement shivered up his spine. This was it: This was what he was waiting for.

Tommy started the game, and for three days, he played it almost constantly. Just before the final battle, he erased it all.

*****

For the next two months, Tommy did not play the game at all. He spent his time watching the birds in his small garden. Every day, his parents ate dinner with him on the patio outside his room. They talked for hours about life, death and world news. Some nights, they played word games or cards.

Tommy was getting weaker, and finally, he knew it was time for him to finish playing his new game.

"Mom, Dad, I want you to watch me play my new game." Tommy said one day as his parents sat with him on his small patio.

"All right, but you will have to wait until the weekend." Tommy's dad replied. Then, with a frown, he added, "Can you wait that long?"

Tommy nodded. "I won't die before I have beaten the game, Dad. I promise."

"Tommy, don't."

The Game

"Mom, it's almost time. I'm tired, and every day, I get more tired."

Tommy's mother stared at her fourteen-year-old son, then abruptly stood up and left.

"Dad . . ." Tommy started, then stopped. "Dad, promise me that after I'm dead, you and Mom will play this game."

"Tommy . . ."

"No." Tommy interrupted. "You have to promise me this. Please, Dad."

Tommy's father sighed. "All right, Tommy, I promise."

*****

For the next three weekends, Tommy played the game while his parents watched. He coached them very carefully on how to set the game up.

"The hero is always TOMY." He told them, "Remember. It's real important. The hero's name is always TOMY." He smiled, "The wizard is always ANGY, and the thief is always RUDY."

Tommy's dad smiled sadly. "We'll remember, Son," he whispered, "We will always remember."

Tommy nodded, satisfied.

Just before the final battle, Tommy saved the game and turned it off.

"I'm tired now," he said, "I think it's time for me to go to sleep."

"Tommy," his mother choked back a sob. She and his father bent over and kissed him, then Tommy's mother ran out of the room.

"Dad?"

"What is it, Son?" Tommy's dad asked, his voice husky with unshed tears.

Tommy shook his head, "Dad, I love you and Mom. Tell her that."

"She knows, Son."

"Yeah, but tell her anyway."

"Okay." Tears ran down his father's cheeks.

"Dad, play the game. Promise!"

Tommy's dad tightened his lips, took a deep breath, and nodded. "We will play the game, Tommy; if it means that much to you."

"It does. Thanks, Dad." Tommy lay back in his bed and watched sadly as his father left the room.

The Game

Tommy lay staring into the darkness as, down the hall, he heard his mother crying softly and his father trying to comfort her. He lay there until his parents had gone to bed and at last, the house was quiet. He sat up, turned on the television and loaded the game at the point he last saved it.

Alone in his room, Tommy fought the final battle.

*****

A year passed before Tommy's parents could bear the face the game Tommy was so insistent they play. They sat next to each other on the couch and turned the game on. Carefully, they typed in the hero's name. TOMY.

There, on the screen, instead of the square computer-generated figure, stood a brown-eyed boy with straight, blond hair and a wicked grin.

The Truth Behind the Madness

"Hey Zondra, what you doing in town? Shouldn't you be at the guardian compound studying whatever you guardians study?"

Zondra laughed, "Joey, you know me, I don't believe all that garbage." She made a face and waved her arms around her head. "Woo hoo! Look out or the big black cloud will gobble you up."

Both young people laughed.

"You going to Charles's party?" Joey put his arms around her and hugged her close.

"Yes. All the other guardians at the compound have gone up to those moldy, old spaceships." She grinned impishly, "Besides, I am afraid of heights."

"Yeah, right." Joey winked at her and, arm-in-arm, the two young people walked down the street to their friend's home.

"Hey, Charles, look who I found wandering the streets." Joey yelled as they entered the house.

"Hey girl, I thought you were going in space today." Charles grinned as he handed the newcomers a drink.

"Why?" Zondra took a deep swallow and grimaced, "Too sweet, and not enough kick. I have the whole weekend off, I intend to enjoy every minute of it." She walked to the bar and exchanged her drink for another.

Charles frowned, then shrugged. Zondra ignored the scandalized looks from the town girls, who stood in a circle by the far wall, with their tightly-braided hair and long skirts. Zondra shook back her flowing black hair, and smiled. Townie women were so restrained and uptight.

She had plans for this weekend and if all went well, by Monday, Joey would never look at another woman. She glanced at him and frowned at the look of distaste she caught on his face. When he saw her staring, he smiled and winked. Zondra relaxed and smiled back. Everything was okay. That look was just a trick of her imagination.

"So, who is going to protect us poor townies from the mean, old cloud if you are partying down here?" Charles jibed.

Zondra laughed, "It's a cloud, what's it going to do? Rain on us?"

"The Little Ones have left." A soft voice interjected.

Zondra frowned, "So what? They probably have some obscure festival to attend. Don't be such a sob sister, Caroline."

"Zondra, the aborigines said they were going to hide from the bad thing."

Zondra shrugged, "How can you even understand them, and why would you bother? They're always running on about some disaster or the other."

Caroline gave her a look of total disgust and walked away.

*****

Zondra snuggled in Joey's arms and stared at the full moon through his bedroom window. Joey's parents were not happy when they saw her. She heard the scorn in the old man's voice when he spat the word "guardian" at her. Zondra smiled in the dark. Joey's father would come around when she and Joey officially became a couple.

She closed her eyes, dreaming of living in town, having normal children, not "special guardian" children. She and Joey would live in a nice home and they would be together forever.

"Joey?"

"Hmmm?"

"When are we going to get married?"

Joey shifted in the bed next to her, and remained silent.

"Joey?"

"Who said anything about marriage?" Joey pulled her close, "I thought we were just having fun. I'm not ready to settle down, and when the time does come, it will probably be to someone my parents choose for me. I thought you knew that."

Zondra winced as the pain of rejection ripped through her. Silently, she got out of bed, dressed in the form-fitting outfit that marked her as a guardian and walked out of the house. For the first time in her life, she felt ashamed by the way the dark blue jumpsuit clung to her slight figure.

Tears poured down her cheeks as she walked alone through the silent night, out of town and toward the guardian compound.

It is so dark, she thought, one second before the alarm horns blared.

Zondra stopped, looked up, and realized that the moon and the stars were gone. The alarms kept wailing and Zondra smiled grimly. *Either this is another of my grandmother's endless drills, or I have been wrong all these years. Oh well, there is nothing I can do about it now.*

Her mood was black as the night as she continued walking slowly toward the compound. *Nothing is going right for me. If only I had been born a townie, a normal person without any mental powers, none of this would be happening to me. Not that I have that much: I managed to avoid all training after I was twelve, so even if this is the real thing, I wouldn't have the slightest idea what to do.*

As she entered the compound, her grandmother grabbed her arm, "Zondra, take that shuttle to the town and pick up a load of townies. Take them to module C, then come back and pick up a second lot. If you are quick enough, we may have enough time to make three runs. That should get most of our people out of harm's way."

Zondra did not move, and her grandmother, Enid, about to enter her own shuttle, snapped, "What are you waiting for? Move!"

"Grandma, I can't fly one of those things." Zondra whispered, and cringed at the look of disgust on her grandmother's face.

"It's not my fault I'm afraid of heights." That sounded pathetic even to Zondra's ears.

"Get in the shuttle. You are going to be taking a seat that could be used for someone else, and I should leave you here, but you may be useful for something later on. Well, don't just stand there, get in."

Zondra crawled in the shuttle as her angry grandmother took the controls, and headed into town.

Zondra slumped down in her seat; trying to ignore the scornful looks of the young people she had thought her friends. Once the shuttle was filled with small children, Enid took off, pushing the large shuttle to its maximum speed.

Zondra sat with her eyes closed until one of the children, a brown-eyed girl in a pretty blue dress, pulled on her arm.

"Lady, are you okay? You can hold my hand if you're scared. I'm not a guardian yet, but I will be one day. I'll take care of you, okay?"

Zondra nodded as tears of shame poured down her cheek. *What sort of person am I? I had the power to protect and abandoned it, while this child who has not yet started her training, volunteers to protect.*

*****

Enid docked the shuttle at pod C and opened the door.

"Get these children into the pod and make sure they are settled, then go to the guardian center. Hurry!"

The Truth Behind the Madness

"What do I do in the center?" Zondra asked as she helped the children leave the shuttle.

Enid snorted, "Make sure all the doors are securely shut," she paused, "If you see any red lights on the command console, let me know. Can you manage that?"

Zondra nodded, then realized her grandmother couldn't see her and answered, "Yes ma'am."

*****

"Lady, there is a yellow light blinking in here." Zondra lifted her head and stared at the girl in the blue dress.

"It's okay, as long as it isn't red."

The little girl frowned, "Are you sure?"

Zondra nodded, her mind back on the planet, her eyes staring blankly into space. She jumped as her grandmother's voice sounded next to her, and then relaxed as she realized it was the radio. She frowned and wondered why Enid left the radio on.

"Caroline, get on the shuttle now!" Grandmother Enid's voice commanded.

"No, Joey, I don't want to leave you." Caroline's voice came over the radio, and Zondra stared in surprise.

"Caroline, I'll join you on the next flight. Go ahead, Dearheart, I'll be okay." Joey's voice was gentle, full of real caring.

He never used that tone when he talked to me. All these years, I have done everything he asked. I skipped my lessons to be with him. I gave up my heritage to be near him, and all this time he was in love with Caroline. What was I? What did he feel for me? Zondra closed her eyes against the pain tearing through her soul. She tried to ignore the mocking little voice in her head that laughed and chanted, *A bit of fun, nothing else; you meant nothing to him. Fool! Fool!*

The radio crackled to life again, this time the voice was that of the Senior Singer, "Enid, what are you doing? We have to leave now."

"I am making one more run, I will catch up, this shuttle is fast, and I'm very good at driving it." Enid chuckled, "Go, go get moving I'll see you in a few hours."

"Where are the children?" The Senior Singer asked.

"Pod C. They have no guardian with them, so be careful with that section."

"Got you. Good luck."

Zondra sat on the floor in the small room, and stared at the door before her. A small frown crossed her face, *I don't remember closing that door,* then she shrugged. *I'll leave it closed. These children do not need to see me huddled on the floor like this.* She wiped the tears from her face and closed her eyes. *Oh, Joey, why couldn't you have loved me? I would have done anything for you; I did everything for you. Ever since I was thirteen, I loved you; I was always there for you. I am prettier than Caroline. She was so useless: Always whining, always looking at me with disapproval. Why did you choose her over me? What did she have that I didn't?*

"Zondra! Zondra! What are you doing? Pay attention, Girl."

Zondra blinked, as her grandmother's voice echoed in her mind.

"What?" Her answering thought was sulky.

"Is everything all right?"

"Yeah."

*****

"Miss, Miss, help us. The room is shaking, the light over the door is red, and a horn is blowing really, really loud. Miss?"

Zondra shook her head and stared at the door, she heard the little girl in the blue dress, her tiny fists hitting the door, her voice filled with fear. The control room shuddered, *how could such a small person hit a metal door hard enough to make the room shake,* Zondra wondered.

"Miss! Miss, help us. Please help us. Open the door. Please, Miss, we don't want to die, Miss."

But I don't know how to open the door, I can't do anything; please forgive me, I can't help you, I can't.

"Enid, did you see what happened?" The Senior Singer's voice came over the radio.

"Pod C just broke loose from the ship." Enid's voice was calm, "I'm going to try and intercept the pod and nudge it back to the ship."

"Enid, be careful."

"Don't worry, this shuttle is big enough and heavy enough to withstand the impact if I time it just right."

The pod didn't fall; I can still hear the little girl in the blue dress. She is still at the door. I hear her calling me.

"Zondra, are you all right?" Enid's mind touch was gentle.

"Grandma, she is still here; the little girl in the blue dress, she needs my help. How do I open the door? She is calling me. She doesn't want to die."

"Do not try to open the door, she will be fine. I'm going to rescue her."

"She said the light turned red, and a horn was blowing. She asked me to help, but I didn't know what to do."

"Oh stars in the heaven, no. Oh please no." Enid's voice came over the radio.

"Grandmother?" Zondra sent the thought across the void of space.

"Enid, what is happening?" The

Senior Singer asked.

"The door to pod C just blew out. The children are dead they are all dead."

"Enid, look out! Enid!"

Zondra screamed. She felt their deaths, all of them, and knew they died because of her: Her grandmother, Joey, Charles, the children, all of them died.

I am to blame for this. They died because of me. Zondra kept screaming while the voice of the little girl in her pretty blue dress cried, "We don't want to die, help us. Help us. Open the door. Help us."

Zondra looked up and saw the brown-eyed child standing in front of her. The little girl held out her hands, bloody from pounding on the door. "We don't want to die. You said it was all right. Why didn't you help us?"

"I didn't know how. I didn't know what to do, I'm sorry. I'm so sorry. Please forgive me."

Joey and Charles joined the little girl, "Never. We will never forgive you."

Zondra cringed at the scorn in their voices.

*****

"Zondra, take this. It is the memory stone of our people. Keep it safe. I love you, grandchild of my heart; I failed you by letting you get away with your reckless behavior. You never wanted the responsibility of being a guardian, I should never have forced you to do something that you were not qualified to do. I absolve you of all guilt and accept all responsibility for what happened. Farewell."

Zondra shuddered; she looked at the pink stone nestled in her hands, *even in death, you try to protect me. Grandmother, I'm sorry I have failed you. I have failed everyone who trusted me. I will see forever that pretty blue dress, and those trusting brown eyes. She did not want to die. Joey did not want to die. Charles did not want to die. None of them wanted to die, but they died. They all died because of me.*

She had no idea how long she sat rocking on the floor. She could no longer scream at the horror of her actions, her voice was gone.

I cannot forget. She will not go away. If I close my eyes, she is there, her bloody hands outstretched. While my eyes are open, she is there, her brown eyes full of tears, pleading for her life, accusing me of murder. She will not leave me; she will not go away.

Zondra curled into a ball on the cold, metal floor, and closed her eyes, willing darkness, willing oblivion.

*****

Where am I? Who am I?

She was in a strange place. Sparkling blue lines crisscrossed the entire area and provided the only light. What she could see of the walls and the ceiling were curved, and looked purple in the flickering blue light. Small wisps of smoke drifted between the lines. One of the smoke wisps drifted into a blue line, there was a small flash and the wisp vanished.

Electricity? Is this the ship? Ship, what ship? Why can't I remember?

Whispers surrounded her, a warning in their touch, "Be quiet; be still. You should not be here. This is the memory stone. Only the dead are here."

"Am I dead?"

"No, not dead, but now you are trapped. You cannot leave here. This place is not what we thought; it is not what we thought. We cannot warn those outside, there is so much we know that we are not allowed to share."

"What stops you? Who are you?"

"We are the spirits of the guardians; we saw the creation of the guardians and the death of our world. Now, we are fading; being absorbed by this stone. Soon, we will be gone and our knowledge will never be shared with others. You are our only hope. You did not die. You are a living spirit. We will give you our memories. One day, one whose mind matches yours will come and you will be free. Tell our people the darkness was not always full of hate: once it was a part of us; but our hate, our greed and our fear turned it against us. We created our worst enemy.

"The stone is an alien thing. It absorbs our powers, influences our decisions and when we die, it consumes our spirits. It feeds on us, on our energy; and it restricts the information that we can give. Study it well; you will see its weakness, learn how to disable it."

"Water would short out the lines, but it would make the stone useless, you would all die."

"We are already dead."

"All of your memories would disappear."

"We will give them all to you. Once you have destroyed the power of the stone, it can be used to store memories safely. It will be a place that the spirits of the guardians can wait for the final confrontation."

"How will I get water in here?"

"We believe in you. You will find a way. You have to. We trust you." The whispers, like wisps of smoke surrounded her, their voices drowning out all of her emotion, overwhelming her senses, suffocating her, burying her identity.

*****

Who am I? Why am I here? A glimpse of blue; tear filled brown eyes, I remember! No! Let me forget. Love. Love and water. Water? What? Who? Where? Help me! Soft hands reached out to her.

"Miss, Miss I'll help you."

I remember, I AM ZONDRA!!

Brown eyes smiled sadly, "We must love: love and accept. Remember. Please, Miss, remember. I'll protect you, Miss."

In a small, dark corner of the memory stone, surrounded by the memories of those long dead, a living spirit huddled shivering, and by her side, stood her protector, a small, brown-eyed figure in blue.

The Madness Begins

"Mommy, Daddy, where are you? My head hurts. Mommy, Daddy, help me!" Anna shook her head, trying to dislodge the scenes running through her mind. *No, I don't want to remember. I want to forget, I want to forget all the screams as my people died around me. I want to forget that horrid feeling as the ship tumbled to the earth, the smell and taste of salt water rushing over me, the feel of cold webbed fingers pulling me away from my parents.*

"Mommy, Daddy, come back, please don't leave me! Why is everyone angry? I didn't do anything. Don't hurt me, please don't hurt me. No! No, I'm only two; it's not my fault. It's not my fault." The screams of fear and anger battered her tiny mind until,

in self-defense, it closed tightly around the dark, empty place where Mommy and Daddy once lived. Anna shuddered and wiped the tears from her cheeks. *I must get away from here. This festival to celebrate our arrival sickens me. How can we celebrate our failure? Have the fish taken our memory away?*

Anna scowled and turned away from the beach. She walked slowly out of the bright city. She hated the city built so close to the sound and smell of the ocean that was responsible for her parents' deaths. She hated the silver, fishy Feltan who let her parents die.

"Anna, where are you going?"

Anna turned, "Oh, hello Em. I'm off to the library. I have some studying to do." She frowned, so much for her privacy. "Why aren't you in the city?"

Em smiled smugly, "I'm meeting someone in a few minutes. Don't you have a partner for the festival?"

Anna shook her head and walked away. *Stupid cow,* she thought viciously, *She knows how I feel about those fish people. Besides, it's not like I could take mate even if I wanted to. I am no Singer. I don't want to be a Singer.*

Her black mood lasted all the way up the hill to the library complex. With a small sigh, she opened the door, stepped into the cool darkness of the large, stone building, lit a lamp and looked around. There were so few books, so little information about the history of the Lantian people. So much was lost forever, so many were lost forever. Tears ran down her cheeks as she remembered the terror she felt when the ships spiraled out of control. Every night, she relived the pain and loss of that day.

She walked slowly to the room in the back and stared at the small, pink orb that was the room's only content. *If only there was some way to access the memories stored there, but no one with the power of mind touch is interested. They all want to forget, to hide themselves and pretend that we are safe; pretend that the nightmare of our past will ignore us. Stupid, stupid and short-sighted, why can't they understand how wrong this is?*

The Madness Begins

Anna slammed her hands down on the table, the pink orb wobbled, then slowly rolled toward the floor.

"Aaah smoke and fire," Anna reached out and grabbed the stone before it landed on the hard stone floor.

YES!! AT LAST!! The words echoed in her head, as pain, burning like fire, tore through her mind. The world around her went black. Memories of a thousand death cries as the last Lantian civilians died, and the tortured cries of the surviving guardians, washed over her. She felt once more her parents' deaths; the attack of the humans who were native to this world; and the brutal mental retaliation of her people.

"I was only two!" She screamed, "I was not to blame." Once again, her mind shattered. Her screams filled the building, and her pain poured down the hill, disrupting the festival in the city below.

The rescuers found Anna curled into a ball on the floor, her eyes full of horror, and her mouth open in a soundless scream. The pink memory stone lay, undamaged, across the room.

*****

Three days later, Anna opened her eyes and stared at the concerned faces around her. She glanced at the Feltan elder sitting near her bed and gave him a twisted smile.

"You will swear to me," her voice was harsh, "You will swear on your mother, the sea, that when my people call, all the Feltan will answer. You will swear that when the time comes, even if it is a thousand years from now, and no matter what the circumstances, that your people will answer our call, even if it means their deaths."

"Anna, how dare you!" Senior Singer Torrey admonished, "It is not your place to speak for the Lantian people."

"If not me, then who?" Anna did not take her eyes off the Feltan. She did not know his name, nor did she care.

The Feltan drew back slightly, then frowned. "She is right. Something happened to her, something that is of your people. I do not understand it, but she has gained the right to demand such an oath from me."

The Madness Begins

He was silent for a moment, then nodded, "I swear upon the sea mother that whenever or wherever your people call, mine will answer, even if it means our deaths."

Anna nodded, then closed her eyes and turned away from him.

"Who are you?" Torrey asked, gently touching Anna's face.

"I am Anna and I am Zondra. I am the terrible truth behind the lies. I am the past, and I have seen the future."

"What have you seen?" Torrey demanded.

"That the dark one will return in a place and a time that you least expect." Anna smiled, "You will weep and you will die, but I will help you win, if you wish it, and I will drive you mad."

Anna opened her eyes, stared at those around her and laughed. The sound made them draw back, horror stamped on their faces. Those who value the power of the mind fear madness more than any other ailment.

*****

Anna spent the next year in the library, writing down the history of her people, as told by Zondra, who had spent a millennium absorbing information from the others in the memory stone. At the end, she saw the full picture of what her people faced.

"We are fighting ourselves." She murmured as she lay down her pen and placed the final volume in its place.

She walked out of the library and down the hill toward the city her people, with the help of the Feltan, built. A small frown crossed her face, "Which one of them do I need?" she murmured. "All these fishes look alike to me."

In her mind, Zondra spoke sharply, "Get past that, right now. We need them. Without the fishmen, our plan will not work. We need them to place their water magic in the stone."

Anna glanced around the area. "There. That male: The one standing alone by the seawall; that's the fool who thinks he is in love with Torrey." Zondra added more calmly.

"Are you sure this will work?"

"It has to. We must convince him to take the memory stone, to use the magic of the ocean upon it. This is the only way to free those held captive by the stone." Zondra snapped. "I have told you this before, why do you hesitate now?"

"I don't wish any more of my people to die." Anna protested. "The anger of the sea will kill all of them."

She felt Zondra shrug. "They are already dead."

Anna shuddered as she walked casually to the sea wall. She stood a few feet away from the Feltan, and stared around with a look of disgust on her face, "My people have forgotten their heritage," she spoke just loudly enough for the Feltan to hear. "Now Torrey is wanting to spend more time in the sea. I hope she drowns." Anna smiled "It's a good thing for the Lantian people that she does not remember the memory stone's ability to hold magic. If she did we would lose her to those damned fishpeople." Anna turned, spat in the water, and walked away.

Do you think he took the bait? She asked the presence in her mind.

Zondra chuckled softly, "Like the dumb fish that he is. Look at him: he can hardly wait to get his hands on the stone. Let us leave the stone unprotected for a while." Anna laughed aloud, as the Feltan hurried past her toward the library.

*****

"Anna, what are you doing?"

Anna turned, "Hello, Torrey. Can't I walk through the town? Would you have me locked up and hidden from the people?" Anna folded her arms across her chest.

"Anna, that is not what I meant, and you know it." Torrey objected. "It's just that you very seldom come down here."

Anna nodded, "I am not fond of this place," she said softly, a faraway look in her eyes. "Don't you remember? I heard my parents drown on this very beach." She turned her back to the ocean.

"Anna, I'm sorry. I forgot about your parents." Torrey reached out to touch Anna's arm.

The Madness Begins

Anna jerked away, "I don't want your sympathy. I want you to listen to what you just said. You forgot about my parents' deaths. What else have you forgotten in the last eighteen years? We cannot forget. Do you understand? We cannot afford to forget, not ever, not in eighteen years or eighty years or even eight hundred years."

"Anna, don't. It's over; there is nothing more for us to lose. The nightmare will leave us be. We are defeated. There is nothing more it can take from us."

Anna laughed bitterly. "We live. As long as even one of us lives, it will find us." She shrugged and turned away, "Never mind. I am going back to the library. In the meantime, I suggest you start remembering."

*****

It is done. The Feltan has taken our memory stone. Even now, he casts the forbidden sea magic upon it. Soon, the wrath of the sea mother will come. In that time of turmoil; open your mind and I will reach out and show all the people their future and their past. I will tell them what they need to do. Zondra's voice was calm.

Anna stepped out of the library and stared out over the ocean. Then she saw it: Tall against the sky, a wave of water sped to the shore. With a small shrug, Anna went inside the library, lay on the floor, opened her mind, and waited.

The sound of rushing water filled her ears. The screams of her people, their fear and confusion buffeted her psyche and her physical body. Then there was silence and the rushing flowed out of her and into the hearts and minds of the Lantian people.

Anna smiled. She had done her duty. The memory stone was gone and the Lantian people would turn away from the Feltan and the sea. But most important of all, her people would remember. When their nemesis returned, they would be ready; they would know how to defeat it. She relaxed and breathed out for the last time. She let her spirit fly free; she was alone now, but soon more of her people would join her.

IL HO A LANTIA.

LITTLE BROWN JUG

Most Famous

"Why did we listen to Kenneth?" I asked Beth, staring at Kenneth's back.

Beth grinned, "Because Kenneth knows everything. That's why we believed him instead of the weatherman."

"God, we're so stupid. Kenneth says, 'everyone knows that hurricanes never develop in the Bahamas in June', and dummy us, we go right along with him."

Beth shrugged. "Well, look at the bright side: He's trapped here with us."

"Oh yeah, right. That's real comforting." I was getting a headache, and Beth's optimistic outlook on life was more irritating than usual.

"Well, be honest." Beth said seriously, "The sky is beautiful and clear. The sea is like glass. We had no reason to disbelieve Kenneth."

"Where do you think 'the calm before the storm' came from?"

George, walking in front of us, glanced over his shoulder and chuckled, "Hindsight, Nancy? Complaining is not going to help. We need to find shelter."

"I want to go home." I moaned.

"What you children doing out here on the piers? You crazy or someting? You don't hear the Storm Lady paying the islands a visit?"

I jumped, and spun around to find a tall, slim, young Bahamian male frowning at us. "Ahh, we were told it was too early in the year for a major storm, that the weather people were overreacting." I felt like a fool.

"What fool tell you that? On these islands, the Lady come whenever she want. There ain't no human put rules on her."

The man stared at us as Beth, George and I tried hard not to stare at Kenneth.

Kenneth turned and walked back to us, "My good man, I've been to these islands many times, and I know for a fact that June is too soon for a major storm." Oil slid along his voice and pooled at his feet. We groaned.

"I's Robert. I was born and raised here, I never heard no fact like that. You is an idiot, but I can't let you American children get washed away. You four better come to shelter with me."

"I'm Nancy, and my friends are George, Beth and Kenneth. We are from Kansas."

"Kansas? You know Dorothy?" Robert gave a sly grin.

I shook my head, "That's just a story."

"I know." He nodded, "Good story, though. I like it. You wan hear a good story?" His white teeth flashed in his nut-brown face.

My friends and I exchanged amused glances.

"How much for the story and shelter?" After four days on the island of New Providence, we discovered that everything had a price.

The young man laughed, "De shelter is free. De story cost is the price of a pint of

Myers rum, 'bout two American dollars. Cheap. You come? I tink your friend back there like this story. We don't go far, just down the road a bit."

I sighed. In four days I had learned that "down the road a bit" could mean any distance from three feet to three miles.

"Oh, come on," George said, "This could be fun."

We followed the young man through the back entrance of the straw market to a small, dirty street that ran along the waterfront.

"Woods Rodgers Drive," our guide told us with a grin. "It named after our first governor."

My friends and I exchanged smirks; the name was longer than the width of the street. Two blocks down, we entered a small, gray bar that stank of fish, rum and lye, and followed Robert to an empty table. As we sat, all conversation stopped.

"You give me the money now."

Beth was our treasurer. She handed Robert two dollars, which he passed on to the man next to him.

"You wait here. De story start soon."

Kenneth stared around him, a sneer on his perfectly-formed lips. "You want us to take shelter from a storm in this small, wooden building one street away from the ocean?" He snickered, "I don't think I'm the idiot here."

The bartender smiled, "Boy, this bar been here since before you were born. It will be here when we all dead." He nodded when the money reached him and sent us a pitcher of warm beer.

"How much?" I asked the waitress.

"Nothing, story time. We give free beer."

"What was the two dollars for?" Kenneth asked.

"Dat for the story man. Rest easy, no hurry."

Robert spoke to an old man sitting in a dim corner, "Old 'Fus, dese here is de young people what come all da way from Kansas to hear your story."

The old man nodded. His bright, blue-green eyes, the color of Bahamian water, danced in his weathered, brown face. He lit his pipe and started to speak.

"My father was a Scot and my mother was part African, part Indian, which made me a born Bahamian fisherman: Stubborn, independent, and proud." His voice was deep and easily heard. The power of the ocean flowed through it.

"My name is Rufus Nathaniel, and when I was young, the small island of my birth wasn't enough for me. I wanted to be rich and famous, to do something that nobody had ever done."

He paused and accepted a drink from the waitress.

The normally noisy patrons of the bar sat silently, waiting for the story to continue. Beside me, Kenneth shifted impatiently. The sound of the wind and the sea drifted through the door, bidding us all to, "Shussh, shussh." The first gentle spattering of rain heralded the coming storm.

"My father wanted me to be more than a fisherman. He wanted me to be a doctor, like the first Hanna that came to these islands. He sent me to the best medical school in Scotland. Well, I knew I was born to be the greatest fisherman in the world. I didn't want to be a doctor, so I spent a lot of time on the North Sea fishing trawlers and very little in the classroom.

"I spent five years in the cold northern waters, and all the while, homesickness was like a black hole in my soul. At last, I could stand it no longer. I returned to the warm waters of my islands, and the fiery heat of my parents' anger.

"Oh, but they were grand people, my parents: Once the anger and the disappointment wore off, they forgave me. My father and I made a deal: I would work on my uncle's boat for two years. At the end of that time, if I still wanted to be a fisherman, I would have my own boat."

A sigh of satisfaction ran through the room; each man there knew the importance of that pact. To have his very own boat was every fisherman's dream.

"Did he keep his word?" Kenneth's voice sounded flat and harsh after the musical lilt of the old man's.

Rufus looked at Kenneth with eyes older than the ocean, then nodded. "Aye, he kept his word, but I kept mine too. Stuck with my uncle, worked harder than I'd ever worked. I had to prove to my father that this was what I really wanted. I had goals: To be the best fisherman in the world, to be rich and famous, and to make my folks proud of me."

He paused; a small, sad smile danced across his face, and the waitress hurried to refresh his drink.

"Bermuda Triangle lay that way," he waved toward the east. "We like to think parts of the Bahamas is in it. Maybe, maybe not." He shrugged, his old eyes young for an instant; full of mischief.

"There was a legend when I was young about a fish that lived off the east shore of Acklins Island. The old men called it the granddaddy of all fishes. They said it was as big as a house and smarter than any two humans.

"Well, I questioned fishermen from Bimini to Inagua. Never met one who had seen the fish, but they all knew someone who had. That was enough for me. Now, I knew how I would reach my goal. I'd catch that granddaddy fish, and all the newspaper and radio people would come to Nassau just to interview me. I was going to be rich and famous."

The rain was deafening in the confined space. The wind screamed like a woman in pain, and the waves crashed against the shore. The small building shuddered.

Beth's face was white in the dim light, and George whispered, "Faust's tormented souls."

Old 'Fus nodded and smiled, paying homage to the storm outside.

He took a drink, then continued. "First, though, I had to get my own boat, so I worked even harder, impressed my uncle with some tricks I'd learned trawling in the North Sea. Finally, my uncle went to my daddy. 'Baccahi,' he said, 'That boy of yours is one born fisherman; it be a shame to make him wait two years for his boat. He done learned all he can from me, even taught me some things. Let him go.' So my daddy gave me my boat.

"Ahh, what a boat. She was the most beautiful thing I'd ever seen, and I named her 'Fortune'. Oh, but I was proud of her. Even to this day, there is nothing in the water more lovely than she was. By September, 'Fortune' had been blessed by Father O'Brian, and I was ready to go looking for my dream."

"Hey 'Fus, you was one crazy man. Dat de middle of hurricane season," a voice from one corner of the room called out.

"I was young!" 'Fus's laughter, like the roar of the ocean waves, crashed through the room.

"Man dat's no excuse, even six-year-old Island girls know better."

"Hey, Simon, ain't you de man who sail out for one last catch, right under Hurricane Donna's skirts?" someone else called as the other men laughed.

Rufus sat back and fussed with his pipe, listening to the teasing laughter of the crowd. I felt as if somehow this was all a part of the story time ritual.

I glanced at Kenneth, "You all right?"

"Yeah. This story is stupid, and I hate warm beer." He pushed his third glass away. I frowned. Poor Kenneth. This story was hitting him hard. Kenneth wanted to be a musician, but his wealthy parents insisted that he go to medical school. That's where we all met, and in a few weeks, that's where three of us would return. Not Kenneth, however, he deliberately flunked all his classes, which led to an awful argument with his father and the old man cut off Kenneth's allowance. His share of the cruise money was the last of his father's money. Life was going to be very difficult for Kenneth when we returned to Kansas.

Slowly, the laughter died down. Outside, there was dead silence as the storm paused for a moment. Rufus smiled at the crowd as though we were all a rowdy group of children, and picked up the strands of his story.

"The Lady of Storms was already picking up her skirts when I left Nassau, and I knew I wouldn't have much time to find my fish. My sweet 'Fortune' took the rough passage like Grouper to the cook-pot, and we made real good time. Aye, we made the fourteen day trip in just ten. I spent the next four days sailing around Acklins Island looking for my fish.

"Well, I was getting low on fresh water, so I sailed into Delectable Bay Harbor to buy some supplies. While I was there, I decided to go visit the local Obeah man and see if he could give me any information on how to find my fish. He was the local witch doctor and nothing happened on or around the islands he didn't know about. If anyone knew where to find that fish, it would be him.

"The Obeah man lived in an old shack about two miles up the beach from Delectable Bay, and after I stored my supplies, I walked up to his place. Inside was dark, smoky, and smelt of dry fish and herbs. The Obeah man sat in the only chair in the room, rocking and smoking his pipe.

"'What you want boy?' he asked.

"'That big monster fish.' I sat on the floor by the door.

"'You don' wan nuttin' to do wit dat debil fish, boy. Why you don' go home to your daddy?'

"I shook my head. 'That's my fish. I'm going to catch him, and take him back to Nassau with me. That fish is going to make me rich and famous!'

"'You jus' one stubborn chile. You don' know nuttin'. Dat fish don' belong to nobody, not even the Obeah gods hab anyting to do wit him. Go home chile, 'fore da storm goddess get you and your pretty lil' boat.'

"'I'm not going anywhere without my fish.'

"Well, I sat there on the floor, and the old man watched me. Neither of us said a word for almost two hours. Finally, the old Obeah man shook his head sadly and sighed.

"'You is sure stubborn chile, but if dis is what you wan' den I tell you. It real easy to find dat fish, all you got to do is call him. I is warning you now, don' ask for nuttin' foolish. Cause when you deal wit da debil anyting can happen.'

"Of course, I paid no attention to the old man. I didn't believe in Obeah or magic. I didn't believe in God or the Devil either. The fish I was looking for was just a fish, nothing more, nothing less. I had to keep believing that or the old man's words would have scared me silly."

Here, Old 'Fus paused, smiled, and added softly, "The young can be very arrogant in their ignorance." I swear he was looking straight at Kenneth, whose face had gone white in the dim room.

"I sailed out of Delectable Bay Harbor into some rough water, but 'Fortune' rode those big waves like a surfer, and pretty soon, I figured I'd gone far enough to cast my net and call this monster fish to come meet his fate.

"All this time, the lines of that silly children's story kept running through my head, 'Fishy, fishy little Ellen call you fishy, fish in the sea.'"

A ripple of laughter ran through the room. Old 'Fus nodded and grinned.

"Aye, I tell you, I felt like a fool standing there on my boat yelling, 'Fishy,

fishy this is Rufus calling,' while the wind and the rain whirled around me like some drunken Goombay dancer."

As if in response to his words, the wind outside resumed its mad howling. The building shook and the lantern hanging from the ceiling swayed, causing shadows to dance frantically across the walls.

"All of a sudden I felt 'Fortune' shudder like she had hit a wall, and I knew I finally had that big fish right where I wanted him. I hauled my net up close and got my first look at that fish. I started believing in gods and devils right quick. That creature was bigger than my boat. His scales shimmered in the evening light like precious jewels. It looked as if some careless giant had strewn a handful of rubies, emeralds and sapphires on the surface of the ocean. I never seen anything so beautiful as that fish in my life.

"I stared at that fish for all of five minutes, then I started trying to figure out how I was going to get it to Nassau. That's when I got a big surprise: The fish talked to me.

"He rolled one, big fish eye my way and said, 'I ain't going to Nassau; neither are you if you don't set me free.'

"Now I had a college education and I knew that fishes didn't talk, but I answered this one anyway. 'We are both going back to Nassau. You're going to make me rich and famous.'

"'You young jackass. I'm the devil, and you thought to catch me with a net? You deserve to get what you asked for; you want to be rich?' The fish shook his body and a shower of gems and gold coins fell around me weighing my 'Fortune' down. 'Now you are rich. You want to be famous?'

"The fish laughed, the red in its scales got brighter, and before you could say 'Junkanoo' he had burned my net and was free. He was still laughing as he stared at me.

"'I promise, you shall be famous.'

"I never saw him again, but he kept his promise to me." A bitter smile crossed the old man's face. "The devil always keeps his promises."

Kenneth frowned, "If you're so rich why are you in here telling stories for two dollars? I don't understand why you're complaining. After all, you got what you wanted."

Rufus nodded, "Aye, I got what I wanted." His voice was soft, heavy with sorrow and regret. For a second the room was silent, not even the outside sounds intruded. The storm was over. The winds and waves ceased their tormented screaming, and the world was again at peace.

"Hey boy, dat two dollars don' 'zactly go to the storyteller. It goes to a fund he started for fishermen who lose dere boats and tings," Robert called out from where he sat.

Rufus pulled a pair of crutches from the dark corner behind him, stood up, and painfully hobbled to the door. He turned then and looked at Kenneth, "Aye, Boy, THIS is my fame, and the price I paid is to never sail my sweet 'Fortune' again." The door closed quietly behind him.

*****

Most Famous

We are back in Kansas now. Kenneth has rejoined us in school, though he is a year behind. We all agree he will make a fine doctor. He is, perhaps, a little less cynical, and definitely a little less brash. He made his peace with his father, and grew up. We all have, since that day in Nassau when we listened to the most famous man in the Bahamas: An old storyteller who, from the waist down, had become what the devil named him; a two-legged jackass.

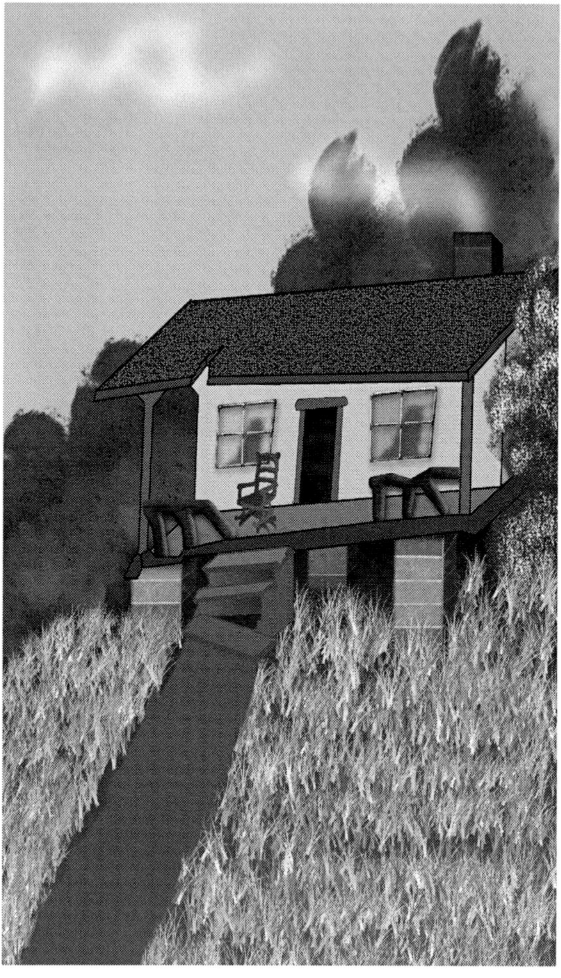

Ida Mae's Rose

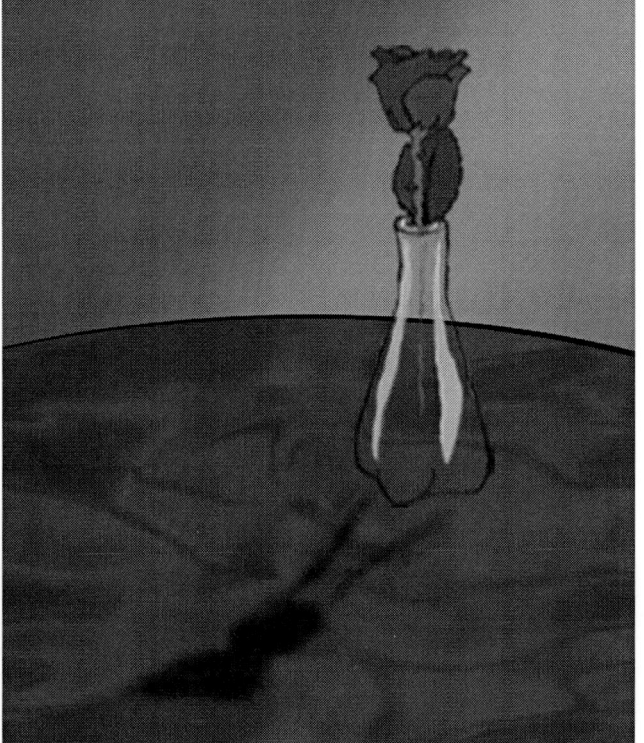

"I hate that Mrs. Cullem. She is nothing but a mean, cranky, old woman, who should have died a long time ago." I slammed the door to the shack Mama and I lived in and stormed into the small, shabby kitchen for a drink of water.

"She has a whole yard full of fruit trees. The fruits are just lying on the ground, rotting, and all I wanted was one, small peach. Didn't give her the right to yell at me, and threaten to call Sheriff Hollihan."

Mama looked at me thoughtfully for a long moment, "Her fruit trees. She can do whatever she wants with them."

"I am not a thief!" I objected.

"Helping yourself to other people's property without their permission is stealing."

I knew Mama would never compromise on that point. I also knew that she was right. With a huge sigh, I walked to the window and stared at the pine trees surrounding our house.

"Mama, I really wanted a peach. I was going to ask, but she started yelling before I could get a word out. I don't care what you say. She's mean and crazy."

Mama looked up and shook her head at me. "Sissy, that's no way to talk. Come here, let me tell you something."

I scowled; the last thing I needed was another of Mama's weird stories. "I have homework."

I hoped that excuse would work. Mama always insisted that I get good grades in school. This time, however, Mama was not going to let me get away.

"Sissy, sit down, now!" Mama used that special tone mothers all over the world use to get instant obedience. I sat.

"Ida Mae Cullem has had a hard time, Child. She was not always an unhappy, old woman; she was a real hell-raiser when she was young. She used to be a fan dancer in the big city."

I grinned at Mama; I knew that a fan dancer was the same as our modern exotic dancer. "How do you know about that, Mama, were you there?" I thought I was being clever by putting Mama on the spot and embarrassing her. I should have known better than to try.

Mama gave me a flat stare and said, "After Ida Mae, I was the most popular dancer in that city.

"Forty-five years ago, she wasn't Mrs. Cullem; she was Ida Mae Bozen, one of the three most popular dancers at the Fantail Club. Ida Mae was not the best or even the prettiest of the dancers, but she was certainly the most enthusiastic. Couple of times, her enthusiasm almost got the Fantail raided by the police.

"Ida Mae got so involved with her dancing, that she would forget to keep her fan up.

"Well, one night, a tall, well-dressed man wandered into the club. He was not at all the regular type of clientele for the

Fantail, he was a real gentleman. He took one look at Ida Mae and his mouth dropped open. He looked as if he had been hit with a poleax. He dropped into a chair, and sat there watching Ida Mae dance.

"When Ida Mae was finished with her set, he sent a note round back to the dressing room. Well, Ida Mae might have been a fan dancer, but she knew her worth. No way was she going to get involved with anyone who hung out at the Fantail. She tore up the note and forgot all about it.

"For the next three months, that man kept coming to the Fantail. He would watch Ida Mae dance, then leave. He never sent her any more notes, but he sent around a bunch of roses every night. Ida Mae asked around and found out his name: William Cullem was from a well-to-do family, and he was a lawyer with a good practice. Soon as she got that information, Ida Mae decided if he sent her any more notes, she was going to take his offer, whatever it was.

"Ida Mae watched for him every night and always smiled and danced extra enthusiastically, just for him. She would give a special little bump and grind, right in front of his table at the end of her routine. He started handing her a single red rose each time she did, but he never sent her any more notes, and he never asked her to join him for a drink. Ida Mae just gave up on hoping and accepted that maybe he just enjoyed her dancing."

Mama frowned, "That man had awful taste in dancers."

I grinned, "Are you still jealous of Mrs. Cullem after all these years?"

Mama snorted, "Never was jealous. I was prettier and I was a better dancer. That was a fact. But I wasn't sweet natured like Ida Mae."

I stared at Mama in astonishment. How anyone could call Ida Mae Cullem sweet natured, was beyond me. "Are we talking about the same person?"

Mama ignored me. "For the next three months, Lawyer Cullem came to every one of Ida Mae's shows. Then, one night, he didn't come. Well, no one thought anything about it, not even Ida Mae, but when he missed a whole week, she got upset. The other girls teased Ida Mae that her lawyer had found someone else.

"It was almost a year before any of them saw him again. World War II was raging in Europe, and Americans were getting edgy, what with wondering when or even if we were going to get involved. Everything was frantic, and the Fantail was doing landmark business. Ida Mae was on the stage dancing when William Cullem walked in. She was so surprised that she about dropped her fan. She stopped dancing for a whole second, then jumped off the stage, shimmied across the room right up to him and kissed his face. With a wicked grin, she ran back to the dressing room.

"After that, things changed between them: Ida Mae still gave William a special bump and grind at the end of her routine, and he still gave her a rose, but now, after the club closed, the two of them left together. Ida Mae said that his parents had died and that was where William had been the last year; taking care of his family business and tying up loose ends. Well, all us girls at the Fantail were worried about Ida

Mae getting hurt. After all, men like him didn't take girls like us seriously, and everyone saw that Ida Mae was getting very serious indeed.

"No one knows how long things would have gone on like that if America hadn't gotten into the war. One night, Ida Mae came into the club wearing a big, flashy diamond, and announced that she and William were getting married the next day and everyone was invited. Well, that sure was some wedding, what with the bride and her friends doing a special version of the fan dance to entertain the guests, and William's snotty-nosed friends and family standing around looking shocked and whispering behind their hands. It was a wonderful party.

"After Ida Mae did her own solo performance, William walked up to her and handed her a beautiful silk rose, 'Ida Mae,' he said. 'I love you now, and I will always love you, I will love you until this rose withers and dies. That is how long I will love you.'

"Everyone thought that was the most romantic thing they ever heard. William joined the Army and went to Europe; Ida Mae kept dancing until the fact that she was in a family way became apparent. She packed up her belongings and went to William's hometown to wait for the babies to be born. The fact that she had twins didn't surprise anyone. Ida Mae did everything with enthusiasm.

"Well, one day, when the twins were about a year old, the servants heard Ida Mae screaming. They rushed into her bedroom to see what was wrong, and found Ida Mae laying on the floor, moaning William's name.

"When the big black military car pulled up outside the Cullem's house, nobody was surprised. They already knew William was dead. You see, when Ida Mae woke up that morning two days earlier; she found her red, silk rose on the floor next to her bed. It was withered and dead."

I was quiet for a moment, then shook my head. "That is the stupidest story you ever told me. It still does not excuse the way she carries on."

Mama pointed silently to a huge basket of fruit sitting in the far corner of the kitchen. "The trees you were after were experimental. She did not know if they were even edible. That's why the fruit was on the ground: To see if the wild creatures would eat them. She sent you that basket; John Paul brought it over just before you came in. Ida Mae is a good woman, don't you forget that, and don't you forget to say 'thank you' next time you see her."

"I didn't know," I mumbled.

Mama smiled, and leaned back in her chair.

"Exactly," she said smugly.

Miss Colby's Stranger

It was one of those hot, still days that are common in the South. Mama and I were sitting on the porch shelling peas, Mama in her creaky old rocking chair, while I curled up on the floor next to her.

"Sissy, if you don't stop eating all my peas we'll have none left for dinner." Mama slapped at my hands.

I grinned at her, "I like them better raw."

Mama just smiled and shook her head.

"Miz Sistella."

Both of us looked up to see Maybelle Crawley waddling down the path to our place. I scowled, and Mama shook her head warningly at me.

"Is somebody sick, Maybelle?" Mama's voice was hard and cold.

"I just thought I'd drop by to visit with you." Maybelle said with a self-satisfied smirk on her face. She turned to me, "Girl, run inside and get me a drink of water."

"No! Sissy you stay right where you are. As for you, Maybelle, say what you have to say and get off my property."

I looked at Mama in surprise. There was a killing hate in her voice that I never heard before.

Maybelle gave Mama a nasty smile. "Well, I was going to do you a favor by telling you that there is some nasty rumors around town 'bout your daughter and that John Paul. You might want to talk to her."

"You can leave now." Mama's expression didn't change.

Maybelle nodded, "Don't say I didn't warn you." She spat and stomped off.

"Mama?"

Mama shook her head, and watched Maybelle turn onto the road.

She sighed, "That woman is poison. She has destroyed a lot people with her vicious lies. The sad part is she knows what she is doing and enjoys it."

"Does that mean I can't be friends with John Paul any more?" I asked quietly.

"You just ignore that woman. I will handle her." Mama touched my head.

"What is her story? She is so mean and twisty, she reminds me of some politicians."

Mama gave her rich, dark-chocolate chuckle, "Difference is, she isn't as stupid as most politicians.

"She don't have a story. Maybelle was born evil. Some people, like John Paul, are born innocent, and then there is Maybelle who is the exact opposite. I remember how her vicious gossip hurt poor little Mary Lynn Colby." Mama shook her head. "I told Maybelle then, I would never forgive her, though everything turned out right for Mary Lynn in the end."

Miss Colby was before my time. She had already left town when I was born, though I did know her brother. Old Man Colby owned the town's only drugstore.

Miss Colby's Stranger

Mama did not approve of gossip, at least, not among living folks. Mama never gossiped with the living because they never got the facts right.

I sighed, took a handful of shelled green peas, and waited for the story that I knew was coming.

"Miss Mary Lynn Colby was the local librarian. She was madly in love with Joseph Forsythe before he joined the Navy. After ten years, Joseph came home and Mary Lynn was at the bus depot waiting for him. When he stepped off the bus with another woman, Mary Lynn's heart broke with a crack heard all over town."

"He should have warned her." I scowled.

Mama nodded. "He was thoughtless. I don't believe he realized how much Mary Lynn loved him.

"Mary Lynn started walking at nights. She would spend most of the night on the hill outside of town, (where the factory is now), staring at the sky. She would come home in the early hours of the morning, swearing that she saw strange lights and heard voices talking to her.

"That's when Maybelle started her campaign of hate she told everyone in town, including John and his new wife all about how, 'poor Mary Lynn had gone crazy with unrequited love of John, and that they should be careful because Mary Lynn could be dangerous.'

"Well, I told Maybelle, to shut up and leave Mary Lynn alone, or she would have to deal with me." Mama smiled, "Back then, I was a force that not many folks in town wanted to cross. Of course, that didn't stop Maybelle, but it made her more cautious in talking about Mary Lynn.

"Most of the townspeople ignored Maybelle. They shook their heads and felt sorry for poor Mary Lynn, who was going crazy with grief and a broken heart.

"Mary Lynn kept going out at night, but she stopped telling people what she saw and heard up there on that hill, though sometimes she would come and talk to me. She knew that everyone thought she was crazy, but she didn't care.

"Well, one morning Mary Lynn, who was no beauty, came down the hill with a handsome young man in tow. She shocked all those upstanding town folks right down to their underpants, especially when he moved right in and lived with Mary Lynn. The man looked to be a good ten years younger than Mary Lynn's thirty-five. Most of the talk in town was from women who wished they had seen him first.

"The young man worked around the old Colby house, fixing things what needed it, and leaving them as didn't, alone."

Mama paused. "That is a rare talent to know the difference between what really needs to be done, and what is just busy work.

"He never spoke to anyone, but he was polite in staying away from all those jealous women who found reasons to stop at Mary Lynn's house. He was especially wary of Maybelle and was always busy some place far away from where she was lurking. Sometimes, you could see him watching everybody with a sad look on his face, as if he knew something that they didn't but couldn't share the information."

Did I mention that Mama had a great imagination?

"Anyway, Mary Lynn brought her young man around to the house one day. 'I'm going to leave this town, soon as I get my affairs in order, Ma'am Sistella, and since you were the only one who ever understood, I thought I would let you know.'

"Well, I looked really hard at that young man, then smiled at Mary Lynn, and nodded.

"'You will be going a long way from home, Mary Lynn, I hope you know what you're doing.'

"Mary Lynn smiled and nodded. 'There's nothing here in this town for me except old age and loneliness. You know who my friend is, don't you?'

"'I have seen his kind before.' I told Mary Lynn.

"'Yes, I thought you might have, that's why I brought him to meet you.' Mary Lynn smiled a sweet, soft smile that made her almost beautiful, 'Wish me happy in my new life, Ma'am Sistella.'

"I looked hard at the two of them, and then gave Mary Lynn a hug, 'You are going to be happy, Girl, you don't need my wish, but for what it's worth, I give it to you.'

"I turned to the young man and told him, 'Listen, you take good care of her. She has never been away from home before.'

"Well, that man, who all of a sudden didn't look so young, turned and smiled at me."

Mama grinned, and for a moment, I saw how beautiful she used to be.

"His smile sent a tingle clear down to my toes, and I knew darned well why Mary Lynn was leaving everything she knew to follow him.

"Mary Lynn went about her business for the next three months, really quiet like, and when the neighbors got wind of what she was doing, it was all the sheriff could do to stop the men from going out and lynching her young man.

"Mary Lynn sold all the stocks and bonds her daddy had left her. She sold the house that her young man had so lovingly repaired; she even sold all her jewelry. Everyone was sure that she was going to ruin her life by giving all her money to that strange young man she picked up on the hill."

Mama shook her head, "You can guess who led the pack. Maybelle was in her glory, running around town, stirring up hate and discontent.

"One morning, about six months later, Mary Lynn and her young man disappeared. The police, and the FBI and everybody searched the area for them, but they were never found."

Mama smiled, "Mary Lynn followed her young man to his home. The search for Mary Lynn and the stranger lost a lot of momentum when the law discovered that all Mary Lynn's money had been put in an envelope and left for her brother, along with a letter.

"Old Man Colby never revealed what was written in that letter, but he said that Mary Lynn was fine, and he called off the search. Of course, there are still people in our town who swear that the stranger murdered Mary Lynn when he discovered that she was leaving all that money to her brother. There are also those in our town who believed that Old Man Colby murdered his sister when he discovered that she was going to give all that money to the stranger."

Mama moved her basket away my hand as I reached for more of the peas.

"I have it on good authority that Mary Lynn isn't dead, though she is no longer on this world."

I raised an eyebrow and laughed. I believed Mama when she said Mary Lynn isn't dead, 'cause Mama would know about things like that, but I wasn't about to encourage my mother in her other strange ideas.

"Mama, that story is ridiculous. Your friends from the great beyond are no more believable than Maybelle."

Mama shook her head, "Well, you are learning. Always question what you hear. Then make your own decisions."

Mama leaned back in her chair, a faraway look in her eyes. "But my version of the story is true. Maybelle's version is nothing but vicious lies."

I thought about what Mama said, then decided no matter how ridiculous, I would believe my mother over Maybelle any day.

Mr. Forsythe's Love

"John Paul, what's the matter?" I was on my way home when I ran into John Paul. He looked unhappy.

"Nothin', I just finish talking to Mr. Forsythe. I told him his garden was sad, and I asked him to let me go take care of them plants, cause I could make them happy."

"So what happened?"

John Paul shrugged, "He yelled at me. Said I should stay out of his garden. I feel really sorry for his plants."

I scowled, "That man makes me so mad."

John Paul smiled, "Now, Little Butterfly, don't take on so. I be doing fine. Mr. Forsythe, he just as sad as his plants."

I gave John Paul a disgusted look. "Now you sound like Mama."

Mr. Forsythe's Love

John Paul laughed, "Well, I gotta go to work now. See you later. Bye."

I watched John Paul shuffle away, then turned down the path to our house. I was graduating in two months, and busy planning my escape from this small town. John Paul had finally received a certificate of completion and he was working as a gardener around town.

Mama was in her usual spot in the old rocking chair on our porch. She took one look at my face and shook her head.

"What are you so angry about now?"

"That Mr. Forsythe…" I stopped, took a deep breath, and started again. "That old man is so cheap he refused to hire John Paul to work in his stupid garden."

I always disliked Mr. Forsythe, the president and the owner of the local bank. He was a sour, self-righteous man, who never smiled, and was so cheap that he squeaked when he walked. Mama told me that Mr. Forsythe had a reason for being the way he was, but I never understood. When I asked Mama how she knew all those things, she just smiled and said her sources told her.

Anyone who knew Mama, knew that her sources were supposed to be from the spirit world, but I found that as hard to believe as I found Mama's stories. In my opinion, the dead should have better things to do than gossip. Mama always asked me why I thought death would change people's behavior. Since I could never come up with an answer for that, I just gave up talking about it.

Mama nodded, "That garden means a lot to Joseph Forsythe. I don't think he would let anyone go there."

I gave Mama a look and she laughed.

"Joseph Forsythe was real popular with the ladies when he was a young man; he was tall, handsome, and good-natured. He always had a smile and a good story to tell. Right after Pearl Harbor, Joseph joined the Navy. That's when he discovered his love for the sea. When the war was over, Joseph joined the Merchant Marines and swore he would never come back to this small, dusty town."

I nodded. I could understand that, I could hardly wait to leave this place myself.

Mr. Forsythe's Love

"Anyway, Joseph showed up about ten years later with a beautiful bride. Her hair was cornflower silk, and her eyes reminded you of the ocean. Sometimes, her eyes were a calm clear blue, and sometimes they were an angry, muddy gray. Nobody could figure out why Joseph brought his beautiful, fragile bride to his hometown, but they all tried to make her feel welcome.

"Joseph built her a beautiful home with large, airy rooms and a swimming pool in the back yard. The builders always gossiped about the size and number of sunken tubs placed in almost every room of the new house.

"Joseph Forsythe planted a garden around the swimming pool. He installed a fancy sprinkler that watered the plants day and night. He built waterfalls, statues of fishes, sea birds, mermaids, and all sorts of fanciful stuff. Inside the house, he hung paintings of fairies and beaches. His favorite, however, was of a mermaid with cornflower silk hair and ocean-blue eyes. As soon as you walked into the house, it was the first picture you saw. The folks in town all shook their heads and swore that Joseph was crazy trying to please that young wife of his."

Mama paused, a faraway look on her face, "I could never understand why they thought Mrs. Forsythe was young. You only had to look into her eyes to see that woman was older than anybody in the town.

"The maids that worked up in the big house always told stories about Amanda Forsythe. She seldom spoke to them, or anyone else in the town, for that matter. They used to shake their heads and say how much time she spent swimming around in the pool, or taking baths, and she always looked like she was crying.

"One day, Amanda came to town. The poor woman was gray; she looked as if all the dust in the town clung to her body. No one had ever seen dust gather on one person like that.

"Joseph was at the bank that day when Amanda walked in and just stood there looking at him, her tears making little white paths in the dust on her cheeks. Joseph looked up, saw his wife, and all the color ran out of his face.

"'Amanda, what are you doing here?' He asked, as he jumped up and ran over to Amanda, holding her in his arms. Well, she put her head on his shoulder and started to cry out loud.

"'Joseph, I love you, but I am going to have a baby, and if I stay here, I will surely die. You must take me home.'

"Well, Joseph Forsythe would not do that, and every time we saw Amanda, she was thinner and sadder. The maids said all she did was weep and say she was going to die if she didn't go home.

"Finally, Joseph and Amanda left. A few months later, Joseph came back home alone. He covered the swimming pool, and smashed all the statues. He sold all the paintings, except one, the one with the mermaid with cornflower silk hair, and calm ocean-blue eyes, holding an infant in her arms. That picture he moved from the living room and placed in his bedroom.

"Joseph Forsythe doesn't talk about his wife and child, or tell stories about the sea anymore. He has become a lonely, bitter, old man."

Mama shook her head sadly, "Someday, when he retires, Joseph Forsythe may go back to the sea to visit. After all, he could no more live in his wife's hometown, than she could live in his, now could he?"

I glared at Mama, "What is that supposed to mean?"

Mama smiled at me, "Whatever you want it to mean, Sissy."

Lost And Found

It had been a bad day and it was quickly getting worse. I peered at my bloody knuckles through swollen eyes and sighed. John Paul walked next to me with his face all scrunched up like he was eating green apples.

"Sissy, you oughten' have started that fight," he mumbled.

"I didn't start it, they did."

"You did so start it. Plowing into ten boys, all older than you, is stupid."

"Well, I sure thought you was going to back me up. Instead, you go running to the sheriff and you tell him I started the fight. I did not."

"You did." John Paul said calmly.

"You heard what they said. I couldn't let them get away with calling Mama names."

John Paul chuckled, "Miz Sistella don't never mind. She always say 'talking ain't doing'."

I started to scowl, then stopped as the pain in my head and face got worse. "If you got in a fight, I would have backed you up."

John Paul stopped walking and stared at me. "Sissy, I ain't smart like you. Guess I ain't smart as nobody in this town, but I don't get in fights. It don't stop no problems; all it do is make folks hurt."

"Go away, John Paul. I can go home the rest of the way by myself. I don't need your help, and I don't need no lecture from you on how to go on."

I kept on walking, and behind me I heard John Paul's shuffling steps. No matter what I said, he was going to follow me home.

As I turned down the overgrown path to the house, I saw Mama sitting on the porch in her old rocking chair, watching me. I flopped down on the broken step leading to the porch. Mama didn't say a word: She just raised one eyebrow and kept on rocking.

"I gave as good as I got."

"Oh?"

"They were saying bad things about you."

Mama sighed, "Sissy, that's no reason for you to start a fight. You want to hurt them? Then you just laugh and keep on walking. How many times I have to tell you? Only start fights you can win." Mama looked at me and shook her head, "Well, you certainly didn't win this one."

"I didn't lose either. Those boys all looked as bad, or worse than I do."

"Girl, not losing is not the same as winning."

"How did you know I started that fight?"

"Sheriff Hollihan came by, told me you was in a fight. Said he thought you were hurt pretty bad. Are you?"

"Got a headache, nothing bad. Sheriff is useless. Instead of chastising those boys, he keeps me out in the hot sun lecturing on about how young ladies don't fight." I snorted, "What world that old man live in? If I waited for some hero to fight my battles, I'd be dead in the street."

Mama frowned, "Girl, you never listen when I tell you: Don't judge people if you don't know their story."

"I know the sheriff real well. He's always lecturing me." I grumbled and stood up.

It was too late. Mama was going to tell one of her ridiculous stories any minute now.

"I remember when he first came to town." Mama smiled and leaned backing her creaky, old rocking chair. "He came by to visit. Said he heard that I knew lots of strange things and that he had a story to tell me."

"Well, at least this story was told to you by a live person." I said under my breath.

Mama gave me a steely look, "Did you say something?"

"No, Mama." I gingerly touched my left front tooth with my tongue. I winced; my swollen mouth was starting to really hurt but at least my tooth was not loose.

Mama sighed, "Come inside and let me take care of your bruises."

"I'm all right."

"No, you are not." Mama snapped. "Now stop arguing and come inside."

*****

Mama tucked me in bed, put cucumber slices on my eyes, and sat next to me. She reached out and smoothed my covers, then leaned back, and picked up her story.

"Girl, big cities are mean places: Lots of people, and not one of them cares about the other. There's murdering, and stealing, and all kinds of nasty things going on. Not even little children are safe."

She sighed. "It takes a hard person to police all the evildoers in the cities. It takes a special breed of human to deal with evil and not be tainted by it. Hollihan was one of the best, but to do his job, he had to close off all his emotions: Anger, hate, love, sympathy, pity, all of them."

"If he was so good, then why is he here?" I mumbled

Mama ignored me and went on with the story.

"The sky was heavy with snow; the air even heavier with dust and smog, when a tall, woman, a pure moonbeam in the gloom, stared at the old brick building before climbing the stairs and stepping inside.

"The large room was uncomfortably warm. Long benches, occupied by skid-row bums and winos, lined the walls to the left and right. Straight ahead was a desk where a bare light bulb glared harshly down on the uniformed man sitting there.

"Sergeant John Hollihan had spent twenty years as a policeman on the beat in New York's Bronx district and nothing surprised him anymore. In his time on the force, he had seen the worst of humanity and learned to live with it.

"That's why, when the young woman walked into the station at midnight on March 15th, he didn't blink an eye. True, she looked stranger than the usual run of young people he saw, but Sergeant Hollihan's only reaction was to wonder when children would ever stop trying to shock their elders with their appearance.

"The young woman had dyed her hair bright orange with black stripes. It rather reminded the sergeant of an old tabby cat he owned when he was young. Her face was cat-shaped, and when she smiled, he noticed her eyeteeth were a lot longer than the others and filed to sharp points. Hollihan wondered idly what dentist had done that job: Surely not a reputable one? He made a mental note to have one of the detectives check it out.

"The woman wrinkled her nose, and, for the first time in years, Hollihan was aware of the air around him, rancid with the scent of unwashed bodies, stale coffee and hopelessness.

"She walked swiftly across the room to face him. 'John Hollihan?'

"'Yeah, that's my name. What can I do for you, Miss?'

"'I am Velvet, and I have something for you.'

"The young woman's voice was husky, with a slight foreign inflection. 'Something that you lost.'

"'Can't be anything important or I would've missed it,' the sergeant said.

"'We found it floating around the cosmos. My supervisor said it was yours and that it was important you got it back. Apparently, it has been missing a long time, so there it is.'

"The young woman laid a small box on the desk next to the sergeant and left.

"Sergeant Hollihan shook his head and stared after her. He could've sworn he saw a long, orange tail swinging under her short skirt. He picked up the box and nearly dropped it again. His arm tingled rather like an electric shock. He set the box on his desk, looked at it for a while, then shrugged and threw it in the garbage."

I heard Mama walk toward my window, "It was eight in the morning when his shift ended. The story of his strange visitor had lightened things up for the men on his shift. He was still chuckling over the incident as he walked to his empty apartment. The emptiness didn't bother him, he liked being alone."

Mama rearranged my covers and sat back down. "When Sergeant Hollihan awoke that evening, there, on his bedside table, was the small box from the night before. As he picked it up, the familiar tingling ran up his arm. *How*, he wondered, as he went into his small kitchen, *did the box get into my bedroom?*

"Sergeant Hollihan would not have admitted it, but he felt a small shiver of fear as he set the box on his kitchen table and stared at it. Something was wrong. He threw the box away at the station, yet here it was in his securely-locked apartment.

"Hollihan wrapped the small box in a towel. On his way to work that night, he threw the box and the towel into a large dumpster."

Mama paused, "Sissy, you still awake?"

"Yes, Mama."

"You feeling any better?"

"Yes, Mama." Now, I loved my mother, and she loved me, but it wasn't something we talked about a lot. It just was. So, after all the work she had done to make me comfortable, I was not about to hurt her feelings by telling her that she actually made me feel worse.

I heard the rustling of Mama's skirt as she settled back in her chair.

"Not even the unusual amount of murders, muggings and mayhem in the city that night could take the sergeant's mind off the strange box. *Why*, he wondered, *am I afraid to open the box? What's in it? Why does that spaced-out female think it belongs to me? Most important, how did it get into my apartment after I threw it away at the station? I wish I could believe that I've seen the last of the box, but somehow, I doubt it.*

"The next morning, Sergeant Hollihan checked to see if his locks had been tampered with before entering his apartment. There was no sign of the box. He was surprised at the twinge of disappointment that shadowed his relief.

"It was as he stepped from the shower that night, and reached for a towel that he saw it again. Naked and wet, his face white with shock and fear, the sergeant stared at the box. He turned and ran from the room.

"His apartment was empty, the locks just as he'd left them when he went to bed, so how had that damned box found its way back to him? He threw the box into the river that night.

"At work, he was grim and tense. His fellow officers kept casting worried looks his way, even the skid-row bums were quiet for once, while they watched him.

"When the sergeant opened his door the next morning, the cat-faced woman was waiting for him with a frown on her face. The box sat on the table before her.

"'I've brought your property back to you.'

"John took a deep breath. Fear, like an earthquake, started in his stomach and sent tremors throughout his body.

"'How do you keep getting in here? Why don't you leave me alone? That thing couldn't possibly belong to me, I've never been to this Cosmos place of yours.'

"'I'm an agent with Galactic Lost and Found. Please, you must accept and open this box. I don't want to fail on my first assignment. It wouldn't look good on my record.'

"Hollihan looked at the woman, and tried hard to ignore the goose pimples that marched up his spine.

"'You're crazy, Lady, what sort of drugs are you on?'

"Why couldn't he shake the feeling that opening the box would destroy his life?

"Velvet smiled. 'Will you open it?'

"'Lady, I'm not about to open that thing.'

"'You have nothing to fear: Not from the box or from me.'

"'What's in here?' He picked up the box and ignored the tingling in his arm. 'I'm not scared. I just don't believe in opening things that aren't mine.'

"'I don't know what's in the box. It does belong to you, though. My boss said it was very important that you have it. Please, at least look inside. If you still think the contents do not belong to you, we will leave you alone.'

Mama stood up and walked toward the door. "What happened?" I asked through swollen lips.

Mama chuckled, her rich, dark chocolate sound, "Why, he opened the box, retired, and moved here."

"Mama, what was in the box?"

Mama opened the door, "Would you believe me if I said it was his lost soul?"

"No," I mumbled sleepily.

"Go to sleep, Sissy." Mama said softly, and closed the door behind her.

I sighed. I hated Mama's stories, and I still didn't like Sheriff Hollihan.

The Butterfly's Kiss

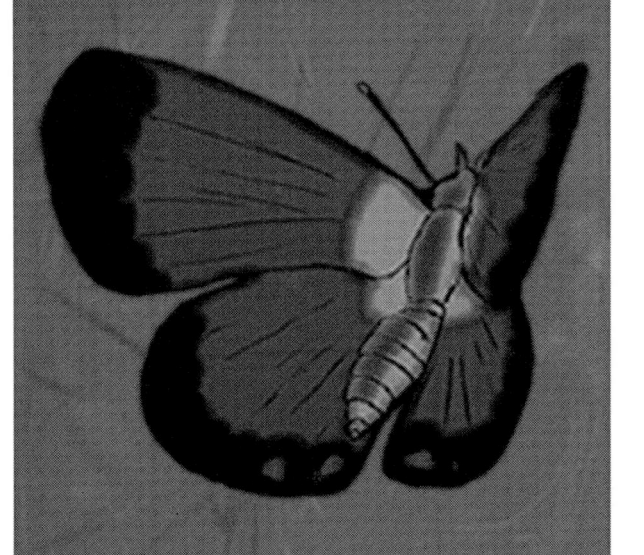

A butterfly kissed me.

The smallest events can change your life forever, even a little thing, like a butterfly's kiss.

I used to be a butterfly trapped in the beautiful, false, crystal world of high fashion and advertising. For three years, Butterfly, my working persona, was a household name. My picture was on billboards and in magazines around the world.

Three things combined to shatter my prism prison: My mother's death, John Paul Jones, and a butterfly's kiss.

I was in Paris when I received word that my mother was very ill. I left, with no regrets, on the first flight out of Orly.

"I'm dying." Mama announced as soon as I entered her room.

The Butterfly's Kiss

"No, you're not. The doctor said that with surgery, you'll be fine." I was used to Mama's ways.

"Not having no surgery. I don't want that boy near me with a knife. He had to be the clumsiest child I ever saw. That's the reason I never invited him to our house for dinner."

"You never invited anyone for dinner because we never had enough to feed ourselves. Mama, you don't know this man. He didn't grow up in town." I was not going to put up with Mama's stubbornness.

"No stranger is cutting me up." Mama said smugly. I had fallen into her trap. "I'm going to join my friends. Only thing I'm sorry about is that I never got to tell you all my stories." Mama sighed dramatically.

All of Mama's "friends" were spirits. Everyone in the small, dusty, Southern town we lived in, thought Mama was crazy and a witch. She would sit on our broken porch and murmur to herself for hours, and even though she never went anywhere, she always knew what was going on in town. No one had any secrets from Mama.

I sat there in that cold hospital room and held Mama's hand while I tried to convince her to have the operation she needed.

"Mama. . .."

"Hush, Child. I have done what I came to do. Now, it is time for me to move on."

"I'm not ready for you to leave me yet." I protested.

"Too bad!" Mama snapped. "I done my duty to you. You are an adult. I don't live your life, don't meddle in mine."

"I love you, Mama." Last try.

Mama smiled. "I love you too, Little Butterfly." She paused, "Remember who first called you that?"

"John Paul Jones. How is he?"

"Dead. He died two winters ago."

"Why didn't you let me know?"

"Why? You were gone three years and never sent one letter home."

"I sent you money." I interrupted.

The Butterfly's Kiss

Mama gave me her 'be quiet' look, and went on as if I had never interrupted.

"You had just started to get famous. You had all your glittery friends around you. I didn't think you cared what happened here."

Mama wasn't bitter or angry, she was just stating what she thought was true. I was silent for a while, thinking about what she said. Maybe it was true. I'd like to think better of myself, but I just wasn't sure.

The first crack appeared in my crystal.

My mind spiraled back to my first day of school. I was all skin and bones, and my hair was not the glorious mop of liquid fire that I have now, but a horrid burnt straw color. I was wearing a dress that was obviously not bought for me: It was too big on the top, and too short on the bottom.

I was six, and as tall as a ten-year-old. John Paul was ten, as big as a grown man, and still in first grade. John Paul and I, we had an alliance between misfits. I was the smartest girl in school, and John Paul was the town's idiot. I was the daughter of a crazy, old witch; John Paul was the son of a worthless, old drunk, and both of us were dirt poor.

Mama called John Paul a 'natural'. She said that a butterfly had kissed him, and because of that, he had the power to understand the speech of all living things. Mama always talked like that.

Maybe she was right about John Paul though. He could make anything grow: He would talk to the plants, flowers, trees, grass, and vegetables, and they would all respond with joyful growth.

I could still smell the day John Paul first called me a butterfly. There, in that sterile hospital room, I smelled the hot, dry earth; the faint scent of rotten fruit; and the sweet smell of the wildflowers John Paul was working with.

I lay on the hot, dusty ground, while my frustration and fury, hotter than the heart of the sun, burned in me.

"How can you be so calm? Don't you ever get angry when those stupid children call you names?"

The Butterfly's Kiss

John Paul patted the dirt around a small plant and sat back on his heels.

"They don't mean no harm. They just speaking the truth. I am slow."

"Well, I don't care." I snarled, "They don't need to be cruel. I can't wait until I'm old enough, I'm going to leave this awful town and I'm never coming back."

John Paul nodded sadly. "I know. You don't belong here. You are so pretty, like a butterfly. You need to be some place green, some place where there is a lot of flowers."

I stared at John Paul in surprise. That was the first time anyone had ever called me pretty.

John Paul smiled at me. "I'll miss you when you go."

"I'll write." I promised impulsively.

"No, you won't. You just be a butterfly and forget." John Paul said sadly.

"Mama," I was back in the cold hospital room, "What happened?"

"The year you left, things got real bad here. There was a drought that summer:

All the plants withered and died. Not even John Paul could keep them alive.

"Then the cannery closed, and nobody could afford to hire John Paul, not with most of them out of work.

"When the new factory opened two years later, a lot of strangers came to town. One of them was a man with a fancy degree in Horticulture." Mama's voice was scornful.

"None of the new folk wanted to hire John Paul. One woman said she was afraid of him." Mama sighed. "People can be stupid. Any of us old residents could have told her that John Paul wouldn't hurt anybody.

"Joseph Forsythe took pity on the boy and hired him to look after his property. With John Paul's help, Old Man Forsythe had the prettiest yard in town, and that made all those new folk jealous.

"The next year, John Paul's daddy died. Now, I know you didn't like Old Man Jones, but you have to admit, he took good care of John Paul." Mama paused and I gave her a small sip of water.

The Butterfly's Kiss

"The old man always made sure John Paul dressed warmly in the winter, and made him eat regularly. Well, John Paul didn't have no one to look after him, and he started sleeping out in Forsythe's garden. I don't think Joseph knew. He would have given John Paul some place to stay if he had."

I snorted, "All Forsythe ever cared about was his bank. He never had any use for people."

Mama glared at me. "Joseph Forsythe has a good heart.

"Anyway, that spring, John Paul started talking about how he had seen the most beautiful butterfly in the world. He said it was all blue and green, and sparkled in the sun. 'Course no one but me believed him. They all thought he was making it up.

"That winter was the coldest in the town's history, and one morning, they found John Paul lying dead in Joseph's garden. He was covered with pine needles, feathers, and fur. It looked like all nature was trying to keep him warm."

Mama smiled, "Strangest thing," she whispered. "On John Paul's bare chest, in the middle of winter, was the most beautiful butterfly anybody had ever seen: All green and blue and sparkling in the winter's sun like emeralds and sapphires. No matter what they did, they couldn't get it off, so they buried him with it."

"A tattoo." I murmured.

Mama gave me her special 'don't be stupid' look. "That's what the sheriff said, but I told him it wasn't a picture. No artist could create colors that bright."

Mama squeezed my hand. "Butterflies don't kiss many people," she whispered, "Butterfly kisses are rare and only very special folk get kissed."

"People like John Paul." I whispered. There were tears in my eyes, though I wasn't sure who I was crying for.

"Don't be sad for John Paul, he died smiling." Mama took a deep breath, "He died with a smile."

We were both silent for a long time, then Mama gave a little cough.

"Mama?"

"Is the sun rising, Sissy?"

I glanced at the window, "Yes."

The Butterfly's Kiss

"Then go and open the blinds. I want to see the sun rise."

I walked across the room and pulled the curtains open.

It was a beautiful morning, the kind of morning you only ever get in America, in the South, in the spring. It was a morning bright with promise, and full of joy.

It was a lie.

When I turned away from the window, I knew Mama was dead. I didn't look at her body. I just walked out of the room, out of the hospital, out of the town.

*****

It's been three years since Mama died, five years since John Paul died. I never went back to my false, glittering world. So far as the people I worked with knew, I just disappeared.

They would be surprised to see me now, standing on a hot, dusty lane waiting for the school bus filled with my very special students.

*****

Oh, the butterfly's kiss? Well, after Mama's funeral, I got on the bus, and, as it drove away from the town, I swear I saw Mama and John Paul, standing by the side of that dry, dusty road, waving.

That's when the small green and blue butterfly kissed me.

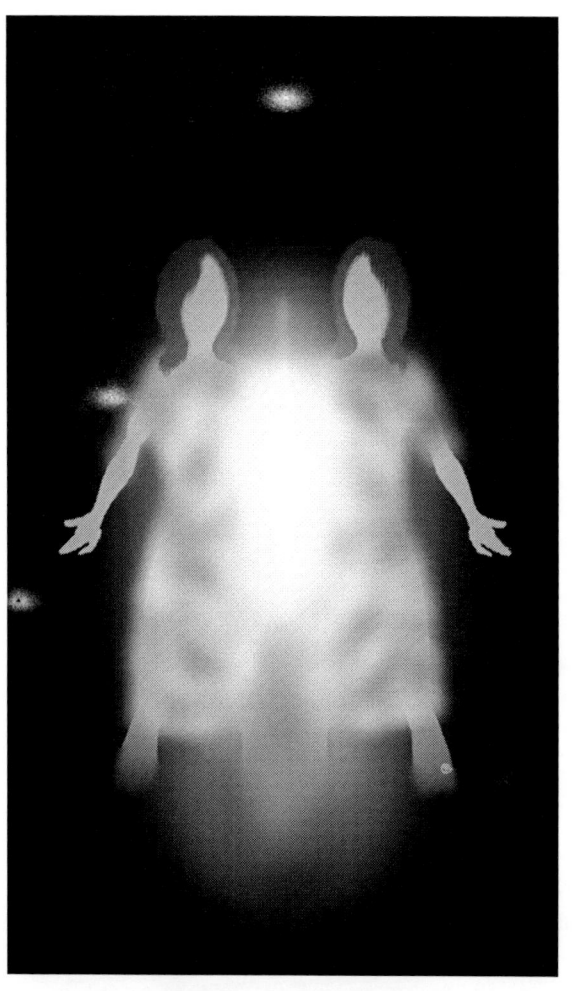

REVENGE

Richard, Sun King of Luith, crumpled the letter and threw it across the room. His wife, Dani-Ta, raised an eyebrow, at this untoward reaction from her normally placid husband. She picked up the crumpled letter and read it.

To my brother, King Richard of Luith:

Long have the lands of Luith and Skarit been friends. Now, I wish to cement that friendship through ties of blood. With this in mind, I would offer my son, Cogi the Golden, as mate to your heir so that they may rule both lands in peace and prosperity. Their children will create a nation unriv-alled in all our world: A nation able to protect itself from aggression by those who would prey upon it.

"Richard, what is in this that angers you so?" She asked quietly.

"It is from my brother, Jos'l." Richard stated flatly.

Dani-Ta, frowned, "How did your brother become lord of all Skarit?"

"Through treachery, just as he achieves every goal he has. Now, he wishes to control Luith through his son."

Dani-Ta closed her eyes and leaned back in her chair, "I must think on this."

"There is nothing to think on. I will handle my brother." Richard answered.

"Richard, you are Sun King through me. I am the moon on earth, I am life and death, justice and revenge, and Luith is my chosen land. A thousand years ago, I promised the Skarit mountain people a place beside me for one of their sons. They are true followers of the moon, and people of honor. If this son of your brother is a child of the mountains, then we will accept him." Dani-Ta stood and walked to the study door, when Richard's voice interrupted her.

far valley. She is not of the mountains." Richard sighed, "My brother married Altha, and through her, became king. When she died in childbirth, he married Goldii."

"What happened to Altha's child?" Dani-Ta asked.

Richard shrugged, "His mother's family took him into the mountains and raised him. That was the last I heard. If they are wise, they will keep him far away from Jos'l and Goldii."

"I did not know that you could hate so well." Dani-Ta smiled.

"Goldii was Altha's midwife." Richard's voice was cold.

Dani-Ta's smile faded. "I see."

*****

The next day, Dani-Ta walked into the study, "Richard, offer our daughter to his mountain-bred son." She instructed.

"No. I will not sign that boy's death warrant, and which daughter will you offer?"

on earth when I am dead. You know the legends as well as anyone."

Richard scowled and turned away "It is of no matter. I have already replied. I refused his offer of an alliance based on one of our daughters marrying his son Cogi. For the good of this land, which you have given me to protect, I will not have my brother in Luith." Richard handed her a copy of his reply.

To Jos'l, My Brother:

There is no way I would allow any child of yours to enter Luith as a representative of the Sun. There is nothing in this land that any other nation would desire, but if it is the will of the gods, then our nation will be no more and no power of man can prevent it.

Your Brother, Richard, Sun King and consort of the Moon

Dani-Ta bowed her head, "Then we shall be bathed in blood and my sons will die," she murmured.

"Nothing." She sighed. "You were not tactful, my husband, but it is done. As was written a thousand years ago, so shall it be. The Sun will decide who will rule in your place. Blessed be."

Richard nodded, "Blessed be the Moon and her consort, the Sun."

*****

She heard the sound of heavy boots and a woman's cry cruelly cut short. She smelled the sickly-sweet scent of fresh blood. She saw the bodies of her family, friends, and servants, obscenely strewn across the floor. She heard a young maid screaming hysterically as she was brutally raped. Lora shuddered, opened her eyes and stared at the ceiling of her room. Each time she tried to sleep, the horror of the night her parents and brothers died, entered her dreams.

I hid and watched it all; watched that young woman who served my family be brutalized. I did nothing. I ran away to the

Revenge

She stood, wrapped her cape about her shoulders, and left the small room that her thoughts and her nightmares haunted.

As Lora walked out of the forest temple, tears ran down her cheeks. *I have wept so much in the last two weeks that I should have no more tears. I am a coward: I hide here and do nothing while my people suffer.*

Her thoughts tumbled, running the same path it had been for days. *How long have I hidden here? Two days, two weeks? I don't remember.* Lora stared blindly into the night. *I can stand this no more. I want revenge. I want to destroy those who have murdered my family.*

She raised her arms high over her head, hands spread far apart, stared at the bright sky and chanted in a clear, cold voice:

"Gray, gray clouds of despair, I call.
Black, black and heavy with sorrow.
Storms cry! Nature weep,
Drench the uncaring earth with tears.
Flood the farms, and the cities.

Destroy joy, banish laughter.
Let the name of this land forevermore be Despair. . ."

"Lora!"

Lora, her concentration, and her spell broken, turned to see her twin sister, Lori, watching from the shadows.

"I want to destroy those responsible for our parents' deaths."

"You don't have the power to do this. Even if you did, it would not be right." Lori whispered. "You would hurt our land and our people with this action."

"I want revenge against the murderers from Skarit."

"So do I." Lori touched Lora's arm. "I was there, I saw what happened. I was forced to be part of it. The only reason our uncle kept me alive was to secure the throne for his youngest son."

"I saw you." Lora's voice was anguished. "I had gone to the meadow to pick the moon-flowers Mother loved so much. When I came in the kitchen, I found you being taken away by the dark, ugly one, and I did nothing. I ran away and hid. I am such a coward."

"There was nothing you could do. If you had come into the room, one of us would have died."

"I should have done something. I represent the dark face of the goddess, death comes under my domain." Lora objected.

"But not yet. Lora, the goddess essence is not yet a part of us. Until we become one, we are powerless."

Both young women were silent, then Lora shrugged and turned away. Lori reached out and stopped her.

"Lora, you have been hiding in the temple since the day of the invasion. Now, you must take my place in the palace. You must see for yourself what is going on."

"Why must either of us go back to the palace? Come with me to the temple. We can stay there until the day of choosing."

"Lora. Our uncle, Jos'l, is holding the lords of Luith hostage to my presence."

uncle. . ." Lora stared at the ground, "I can't do it."

"One of us has to be there. Both of us cannot abandon our people." Lori said sternly.

"Then you go back. Our uncle has dealt with you since. . ." Lora paused, and swallowed hard. "Lori, he would notice the difference." Even as she spoke the words, Lora realized how cowardly she sounded.

"How? We are identical in looks. Even our voices are the same. Besides, he doesn't even know you exist. Don't you think I need a break? I have to get out of the castle, Lora. I need time to commune with the gods, and I need to find peace in my heart before the joining."

Lora bowed her head in shame, "Lori, you are a gentle soul. I am not. Jos'l would have to be a fool not to notice the difference. Our uncle is many things, but he is no fool."

"You want revenge?" Lori asked.

"Yes." Lora answered.

"None who ride with our uncle is innocent!" Lora spat.

"You are wrong." Lori frowned. She looked at her sister's face and sighed. "You do not believe me. You must see it for yourself. Lora, are you willing to pay the price of our revenge?"

"Why should there be a price?"

"The goddess warned Mother, but Father could not believe his brother capable of such treachery. If we want vengeance, we must pay the price."

Lora was silent, then she nodded firmly, "Whatever the price, I will pay."

Lori smiled, "As will I."

"So what do the gods charge for vengeance these days?"

"Lora, remember, it is written that one of Skarit's sons will rule in the land of Luith as Sun King."

"Not one of Jos'l's sons." Lora protested.

"Yes. There is one who found no honor or joy in the massacre of our family."

"Those of Skarit's mountains know honor; they worship the gods faithfully. Only the people of the valley follow our uncle. Go to the palace and speak to the spirits of our family that still linger. There are memories that you must face, or else the bitterness in your soul will destroy our land."

Lora stared stubbornly at her twin.

Lori sighed, "It will not be for long. In three days, there will only be one of us," Lori paused, "And Lora, try to keep your temper under control."

"All right, I will do as you say." Lora agreed slowly.

Lori smiled, and opened her arms. The sisters shared a brief hug.

*****

Lora walked into the castle, ignoring the lewd looks the guards gave her. She went up the stairs to the room she once shared with her twin.

She sighed and sat on her bed, *now I find out my true worth. Lori stayed here for*

Revenge

destroy Skarit and all who live there, but Lori is right: The mountain people deserve a better leader than my uncle.

With a heavy heart, she dressed for dinner. *I hate Lori's choice of colors, but if I don't wear these silly clothes, Uncle Jos'l will notice the difference.* Slowly, her light brown eyes downcast, Lora walked into the dining room and took her seat.

"You are late." Jos'l said sternly.

Lora ignored him, taking great care placing her napkin on her lap. She breathed deeply, and stared at her plate.

"Your aunt and I are holding memorial service for your family tomorrow morning. You will be there." Jos'l ordered.

Lora felt hot anger race through her body. She knew her face was red, and under the table, she clenched her fists so tightly her nails cut into her hands.

"Did you hear me, girl?" Jos'l frowned.

"I hear you, Uncle." Lora whispered, and Jos'l nodded his satisfaction.

stretched tightly over her bony frame, and her eyes cold as only blue eyes could be. His elder son, Boron, was a hard, scarred warrior. His muscular frame, dark hair and eyes, proclaimed him a true son of Skarit's mountains. The younger son, Cogi, was a spoiled petulant child with blond hair and a pretty face.

How can they sit so casually at this table, still stained with the blood of my murdered family? I can't take this, watching them eat, drink, and carry on as if they are honored guests at this table. How dare Jos'l plan a memorial for those he murdered? How dare he pretend to be a loving, grieving brother to the man he slaughtered? I will not go to Jos'l's service. I don't care what he says or does, I will not be there tomorrow.

With a choked, "Excuse me." Lora fled the dining room. Back in her own room, she flopped down on her bed and cried herself to sleep.

she grieved for her family, M*other, Father, farewell. Rest in the arms of the gods.* She prayed. *The old moon is dead. Soon, the new moon will rise. Grant that Lori and I rule as wisely as you.* She sighed, *Lori is so much braver than I. Everyone thinks she is soft and submissive, but there is steel in her; a steel that would make the finest sword. She would bend but never break. My stiff-necked pride would break me. I am death. Dying is easy. Lori is life, and life is much more difficult.*

At peace with herself at last, Lora returned to the castle and prepared for dinner. She wore her own clothes, and walked into the dining room with defiance in every line of her body.

She saw Jos'l watching her with a frown on his face, and knew he sensed the difference in her. If she caused trouble today, he would kill her. Jos'l thought his son could rule Luith without her. He did not believe the prophecies.

You did not show up for the memorial ceremony I held in honor of your parents. Where were you today?"

"Unnatural brother, you murdered your brother for power." Lora's voice was strained.

In her mind, she heard the laughter and the crude jokes of the soldiers as they murdered her family. She saw her father and two brothers sprawled across the dining table, their blood slowly dripping to the floor, staining everything it touched.

She saw her mother, her silver gown torn and stained black with her own blood, while her gentle twin, Lori, was forced to stand beside Jos'l and watch it all.

Lora's eyes narrowed, *not all of the soldiers laughed, there was one. . . * She glanced around the table. *There, that one: Boron. I remember now, he had a look of disgust on his face, as if the whole thing sickened him. He saw me. He looked right at me, then looked away, out the window. What game does that one play?*

my memories. I realize now that a large part of my anger was at myself. I hid in safety while Lori endured. I still feel that I should have been able to do something to free my sister and save my family.

"Girl, pay attention when I speak to you." Jos'l's voice broke into her thoughts. "I left you alive. Don't make me repent my generosity."

Lora lowered her eyes so that he would not see the hatred in them. "You have kept me alive for your own reason, Uncle. Generosity had little to do with it."

Her uncle smiled cruelly, "You think you know me so well? I can be a very generous man to those who please me." He paused, waiting for a reaction from her. When Lora remained silent, he shrugged and continued eating.

Lora stared at the food in front of her and felt the gorge rise in her throat. She forced herself to drink a small sip of wine, then spent the rest of the meal rearranging the food on her plate.

Lords of Luith. In two days, they will meet and choose my son, Cogi, to be the new Sun King. You will be there to stand at his side."

Lora kept her head bowed. "I wish permission to spend the night before the choosing in the Temple Of the Moon." She was furious at having to ask this Northern creature for permission to visit her own temple.

Jos'l nodded, "Take your Aunt Goldii with you. She was trained by the priestesses in the Mountains of Skarit."

Fear slithered down Lora's spine. If Goldii was a Skarit Priestess, why had she not told her husband the true nature of Luith's rulers?

Until tomorrow night, she and Lori were vulnerable. Separately, they were only two helpless young women barely twenty years old. Her uncle could still kill one of them and give Luith to whichever of his sons he wished. After the ceremony that would make them one, the twins would

Lora spent the next day in her room, gathering the few things she needed to take to the temple with her, and wondering how much Goldii told Jos'l.

"Mother," she whispered, "You died too soon. Lori and I are not prepared for this. We should have had years more as sisters; years more of training. If you foresaw this, as Lori claims, why didn't you take steps to avoid it?"

As Lora sat on her bed, a thin circlet of moon silver clasped in her hands, she heard her mother's voice whisper in her heart.

"Lora, your father was the Sun King, but he was no warrior. He was a scholar. We all loved him for his gentle ways, but he did not believe his brother would betray him so cruelly. Forgive him. The one thing we loved most in him destroyed us."

Lora bowed her head and bitterly acknowledged the truth of her mother's words.

*****

to the temple. I would spend the night making my peace with my Lady, and asking her guidance for tomorrow."

Goldii set down the book she was studying, "Did my husband tell you I used to be a priestess in the Skarit Temple?"

"Why did you not tell your lord the truth of Luith?"

Goldii shrugged, "I obey the will of the Lady we both serve."

"The Lady did not sanction the brutal murder of my family, Skarit Priestess."

"You presume to second-guess our Lady? The people of Luith have always been arrogant in their belief that the Moon takes human form to rule over them. Well, my husband has proved that the rulers of Luith are not gods, only mortals, who can bleed and die like the rest of us." Goldii smiled coldly, "Do you think of yourself as the goddess now that your mother is dead?"

When Lora did not answer, the older woman continued. "I have seen, in my

Lora was silent. Goldii stared at her for a moment, then walked out of the library. She returned half-an-hour later with a small basket on her arm.

"Come, Child, I am ready to leave now."

Lora nodded and followed the woman out of the palace and through the gardens, following the path that led to the gates.

"Why didn't you just ask my parents for a marriage? Why come with an army, bringing death to the land of the Moon?" Lora asked after a long silence.

"My Lord sent a letter offering our Cogi as your mate. Your parents refused to even consider him." Goldii's lips firmed. "Your father said that he would see his daughter dead before she was mated to any of Jos'l's young wolves."

Goldii glanced at the young woman walking beside her. "I suggest, in your prayers, you ask our Lady's pardon for your questioning of her will."

important night, and it was vital that all thoughts of anger and revenge be erased from her mind. She would deal with her father's family tomorrow.

"Come, Priestess of Skarit, Queen of the North. It is time you meet the Lady as we worship her in the South."

"Lora, you're going the wrong way."

"No, Aunt. We do not go to the temple in the city. Tonight, we go to the old temple in the forest. Don't worry, you'll be safe as long as you do as you're told and don't interfere."

The old Temple of the Moon stood in a large clearing deep in the forest of Cau. It was a small building that gleamed pure silver in the light of the crescent moon. No sign of the passing years showed on the building: It could have been built one year, or a thousand years ago.

The path to the door was lined with the senior priests of Luith. On the left, stood the fifty ladies-in-waiting to the Moon

"Stay here until someone comes for you." Lora warned, as she dropped her cloak to the ground and removed her shoes.

The followers of the gods bowed their heads as Lora passed them, then fell in line behind her, forming a procession that slowly made its way into the temple. The large, ornate door closed soundlessly behind the last of the priests and Goldii was left alone outside.

Almost an hour later, one of the priests came to lead Goldii into the temple.

"Do you know who I am?" Goldii asked him angrily. "How dare you leave me out here alone all this time? My husband will hear about your rudeness to me! He gave instructions that I was to stay with the princess."

"Sister in the Moon, I am Pak. Welcome to the home of the Goddess on this earth." The priest ignored her tirade as he led Goldii into the temple.

"Pak, where is the princess? Take me to her at once." Goldii demanded.

of the North. The one you seek is no more. The old moon is dead. Now is the day of the new moon. Blessed be our Lady."

Before Goldii could respond, Pak disappeared down the dark corridor.

*****

Deep in the heart of the Temple, Lora and her twin, Lori met.

"It is time. Are you ready?" Lori hugged her twin.

"Boron did not take part in the slaughter. He saw me that night and said nothing."

Lori nodded, "I know. He is the son of prophecy."

"He is still our uncle's son." Lora protested.

Lori smiled, "And blood will tell?"

Lora sighed, "Something like that."

"You know better." Lori chided.

"Yeah." Lora sighed again and watched the priests move towards them. "Who will be dominant?"

"I will miss you." Lora said softly.

Lori stared at her, "Silly, we will still be together. I'm not going anywhere. I will be part of you."

The sisters undressed, and stood while the priests of the Sun and the Moon draped heavily-embroidered shawls around the girls' shoulders. The patterns represented the power of the gods and the silver and gold threads shone in the dim light of the temple. Hand in hand, they approached the twin altars. For a long minute, Lora and Lori were bathed in a brilliant white light. When the light faded, only one remained. In the presence of the Priestesses of the Moon and the Warrior Priests of the Sun, Lora-Ri was born, fulfilling the words of the gods:

> *Twin girls will be born to the Moon queen. When the old queen dies, the twins will become one and a new queen will be born who holds the essence of the Goddess, and rules Luith in the Moon's name.*

*****

aunt awake, "Come Skarit woman, the choosing must be done at the sun's zenith. We must hurry if we would reach the castle in time."

"How dare these priests treat me the way they did?" Goldii snapped. "I promise my husband will hear of this and they shall suffer for their insolence."

"Do you enjoy death so much, that you would bring it upon innocent priests to soothe your wounded feelings?" Lora-Ri glanced over her shoulder at the older woman and kept walking.

"Be careful how you speak to me, or I will have you and those precious priests of yours put to death. Once my beloved Cogi is crowned Sun King, we will have no use for you." Goldii warned.

Lora-Ri smiled grimly, "Be silent, woman. You are a fool, and of no consequence."

Ignoring her aunt, Lora-Ri walked bare-footed through her city and into the great temple at its heart. She walked into the pointed brown face, which was surrounded by long, straight, blue-black hair. She was the goddess in human form, and today, revenge would be hers. With a grim smile on her face, she looked around.

Her uncle and his sons stood on the dais beside the Sun Throne. The Lords of Luith sat at a long table on one side of the room. Jos'l's soldiers stood with drawn weapons, behind the silent lords.

"Niece, I wondered if you were going to miss the ceremony." Jos'l smirked at her.

Lora-Ri ignored her uncle, and stared at the two young men standing beside him. The older son, Boron, was dark and forbidding. His warrior's leathers were brown, and a plain, well-used sword hung at his side. He was all darkness and shadows.

The younger son, Cogi, was the exact opposite: He was a golden man. His armor was made of beaten gold. Around his waist was an ornate sword studded with precious gems, and a small circlet of gold

Lora-Ri's eyes lingered on the younger son for a moment, then she glanced at her uncle.

"Will the choosing be by the customs of Luith?"

"Of course."

"Then why all the soldiers? We have offered no resistance. What makes you think that we would start now?"

Her uncle laughed, "They are here just in case you and your lords decide to object. Don't tell me the thought of revenge never crossed your mind? I would find that hard to believe. After all, you are my niece."

Lora-Ri bowed her head, "My father was your brother."

"Yes. Every family has its weaklings, but you are more my niece than your father's daughter. There is strength in you, Girl, that you have tried to keep hidden. I think now, that I should have killed you." Jos'l murmured to her.

Lora-Ri's body stiffened. She forced herself to relax, and turned to her people.

revealed: A just man with a kind heart, a strong warrior." She swallowed the bitterness in her throat.

"The Lady has promised my mate will be one who can train and protect our people. There will be no foreign invasions while he rules beside me, and the land will prosper."

Jos'l grabbed Lora-Ri's arm, "Wait a minute, Girl. That's not how it's going to be. Who gave you the right to speak in here?"

"The right, Uncle, is mine by birth." Lora-Ri pulled free of his hold, "Didn't your wife tell you? The Sun King lives through me; I die, he dies; I live, he lives. The Moon is queen in this city, Uncle. The Sun King is only her consort."

"Maybe that's how it used to be, but starting right now, that rule is changed." Jos'l's face was red with anger.

Lora-Ri ignored him. He was no longer important. Nothing he said could change the outcome.

sit upon it?"

Her uncle stared at her for a long moment as if suspecting a trap, but unable to see where it was. He glanced at his soldiers, then at his wife, who was standing in the back of the room, a small smile on her face. He frowned briefly, but Goldii nodded impatiently.

"Cogi is my youngest. I think it appropriate that my golden boy should be the new Sun King."

"What if the Lady wants your other son?" Lora-Ri asked quietly.

"Boron." Jos'l spat, "He's worthless. His mother's people have stuffed him full of ideas unworthy of a Skarit warrior. He should have stayed in Skarit's mountains. Cogi is a better choice. Don't you agree?"

Lora-Ri let her eyes linger on the bright form of Cogi for a moment, then shrugged. "The decision, as you have reminded me, Uncle, is yours to make."

Her uncle nodded, and gestured for his younger son to sit on the throne of the

the dais to sit in the large, wooden chair.

The room suddenly became still. A heaviness descended in the room that made breathing difficult. Slowly, the section of roof over the throne rolled open. The sun, at its height in the sky, sent one powerful ray through the opening and bathed the figure sitting there.

The light curled around Cogi, and was reflected to every corner of the room, blinding the watchers. Golden sun, golden hair, the gold chains and the ornate sword Cogi wore, all generated the heat and power of the sun itself. Suddenly, the figure in the chair blurred, the watching soldiers gasped, and Goldii's scream rang out.

Jos'l lurched forward to pull his son away from the throne, but he, too, was caught in the brilliant light. For a heartbeat, no one moved. Lora-Ri lifted her arms and slowly, the roof closed, leaving two boneless lumps of flesh quivering and moaning on the floor before the throne.

what is left of Jos'l and Cogi back to the cold North Lands. Give their care to the healers of Skarit's Mountains."

"What, who, are you?" Goldii stared at Lora-Ri with terror in her eyes.

"I am Lora-Ri the twin heir to Luith's Moon Throne. I am death and life, vengeance and justice. Do you not recognize me, false priestess?"

Goldii covered her face, "Then the myths of Luith are true?" she moaned.

Lora-Ri nodded, a half-smile playing on her face, and the goddess in her spoke to Goldii.

"I have always ruled Luith, for this is my home. Let your eyes be opened my Skarit Priestess. You have let your ambition blind you to the truth. You have willfully ignored the teachings of your religion. Now, the price must be paid."

Goldii fell to her knees, "My Lady, forgive me. It was all my idea. I wanted Cogi to rule as Sun King. He was so bright

"One of your sons will be spared, for it is written that a son of Skarit will sit upon the Sun Throne." Lora-Ri turned away, then stopped.

Goldii stared at Lora-Ri in horror, "I have only one son," she screamed. "That one's mother was some savage mountain princess that Jos'l married before he met me." Goldii pointed at Boron, her face ugly with hatred.

Lora-Ri sighed, "We know the folk of Skarit's Mountains well, Goldii. Their ways may not be ours, but they are no savages. They worship the Lady of the Moon more faithfully than you. Go back to your cold northern land. Take what is left of Jos'l and Cogi with you. You will rule in Skarit until my son is old enough to take control of his birthright."

"You would choose the son of a barbarian over mine?" The older woman asked angrily.

Lora-Ri felt the goddess in her become impatient, "Goldii, you refused to forever any hope of promotion within the temple, so you left and seduced the northern king, Jos'l, away from his wife.

"But that did not satisfy your ambition. Out of spite, you plotted to destroy the land that the Lady you no longer worshipped, held dear." Lora-Ri watched Goldii with a small, cold smile, "Your golden boy and your husband have paid for your ambition. The son of the woman you wronged will sit upon the throne you coveted for your own son."

Bitterly, Goldii gave her husband's soldiers orders to carefully prepare what was left of the two men for transportation to their home.

Boron stared at the featureless lumps of humanity that were once his father and brother, then glared at Lora-Ri.

"You are my father's niece." His voice was cold.

Lora-Ri shrugged, "A debt must be paid."

"Once your brother sat on the Sun Throne there was nothing I could have done. He was not the chosen one. He did not have strength to hold the power he sought."

There was silence as Boron and the people of Luith watched the northern soldiers remove the bodies of Jos'l and Cogi from the Choosing Chamber. Once they were gone, Boron turned to Lora-Ri.

"So now I suppose you want me to sit on that accursed thing?"

"Are you afraid?"

"I'd be a fool not to be."

Lora-Ri nodded, "You are not a fool, but you are the chosen one by the gods and by the people."

"I don't need your Sun Throne, I have a throne in the north waiting for me."

"If Goldii does not rule Skarit wisely, your mother's people will take control."

"What do you know of my mother's people?" Boron asked angrily.

Lora-Ri stepped forward, "Son of Skarit's Mountains, this is your destiny, and the price that honor demands. You did not warn us of your father's treachery. You must rule the land of the gods as Sun King, and protect the people of Luith with your life, if necessary. You have been chosen."

"By whom?" he snarled, "Did you choose me over my younger brother? Did you want me so badly that you had to destroy two members of my family to get me?"

Lora-Ri stiffened, "Want you? If the choice was mine, I would have all of you dead. Your family murdered my parents and my brothers. At least your father and brother are still alive." Lora-Ri took a deep, calming breath, "There are many things between us, Boron of Skarit, and over the years, we will have to deal with them. This union will not be easy, but it is our destiny. Maybe some day, we will find joy together if we both work hard at it. Are you willing to try?"

"Do I have a choice?" Boron asked.

Boron sighed, "My honor demands that I stay in Luith. My family owes your land a king."

Lora-Ri nodded, "Boron, you have been chosen by the children, blessed is the joy of youth. The Sun King is their Protector.

"You have been chosen by the old, blessed is the wisdom of age. The Sun King is their Champion.

"You have been chosen by the workers of the land. Blessed are the fruits of their labor. The Sun King is their Lord.

"You have been chosen by the mortal Lords of the Land. Blessed are they who represent the gods in thoughts and deeds. The Sun King is the holder their honor.

"When your family slaughtered mine, you protested their lack of honor. The dead of Luith have chosen you. Blessed is the peace of death. The Sun King is their Judge.

from Skarit's bleak mountains to sit upon the Throne of the Sun.

"Let the one named, take the throne. Boron, son of Skarit's Mountains and of the cold North, bask in the warmth of the southern sun."

Boron took a deep breath, removed his sword, and sat on the Throne of the Sun. The roof opened once again and the bright light of the sun poured through and flowed over the seated figure of Boron. Lora-Ri stepped forward and placed her hand on his shoulder. The light enveloped them both and reflected a rainbow that arched back out through the open roof and spread over the land of Luith.